When Charles Landon dies, the legacy he leaves behind has very different implications for each of his four children. For sophisticated GRANT LANDON it means that CRISTA ADAMS, his ward, is more than he'd bargained for! What *all* of the Landons find through Landon's legacy, though, is the key that finally unlocks their hearts to love....

Dear Readers,

Welcome again to the exciting world of the Landons, and to the legacy that changes the lives of an entire family.

The idea for these books came to me when a friend and I met for lunch at a restaurant in New York. I overheard some women talking at the next table. They were discussing what makes a man exciting. "He has to be gorgeous," said one. "And a rebel," said another. "And not the least bit interested in being tamed," said a third. The next thing I knew, Cade, Grant and Zach Landon sprang to life inside my head. They were certainly handsome, rebellious and untamable, and when I wondered what kind of women could possibly put up with them, their beautiful sister Kyra materialized and said, well, she'd always loved them, even if they were impossible!

This month, let me introduce you to Grant Landon in *Guardian Groom*. Grant's a New York attorney. Master of any situation, he's never at a loss...until he finds himself the unwilling guardian of Crista Adams, who has the face of an angel and the soul of a gypsy.

Settle back and enjoy four months of love, laughter and tears as you discover the full meaning of the Landon legacy.

With my warmest regards,

Sandra Marton

SANDRA MARTON

Guardian Groom

Harlequin Books

TORONTO • NEW YORK • LONDON
AMSTERDAM • PARIS • SYDNEY • HAMBURG
STOCKHOLM • ATHENS • TOKYO • MILAN
MADRID • WARSAW • BUDAPEST • AUCKLAND

ISBN 0-373-11813-9

GUARDIAN GROOM

First North American Publication 1996.

Copyright © 1995 by Sandra Myles.

This edition published by arrangement with Harlequin Books S.A.

® and TM are trademarks of the publisher. Trademarks indicated with
® are registered in the United States Patent and Trademark Office, the
Canadian Trade Marks Office and in other countries.

Printed in U.S.A.

PROLOGUE

IT WAS late on an unseasonably warm Friday afternoon in September, and all was right in Grant Landon's world.

The deal *The New York Times* had called "impossible" was almost wrapped up, the weekend stretched ahead, and tonight a long-legged beauty whose face graced half the magazine covers in the city was dining with him at his Fifth Avenue apartment—which didn't dim his growing interest in the blue-eyed blonde seated on the other side of his desk.

They had been dueling for the past several hours, each trying to gain the upper hand, but Grant knew better than to allow his attention to be diverted by something other than the intricacies of contract law. Now, with the deal concluded, he could see that she was all the diversion one man could handle.

Alicia Madigan was bright, sophisticated, and coolly elegant. A woman to his liking—and Grant knew just the way she'd like to be handled. A shadowy smile curved across his mouth at the thought, softening the hard, handsome lines of his face.

The Madigan woman noticed.

"Don't look so pleased with yourself," she said lightly. "I'll begin to worry that I gave away too much."

Grant laughed softly. "Come now, Miss Madigan. You know what they say about the fine art of negotiating. You give some, you get some."

She smiled, sat back, and crossed her legs. Her demure suit skirt inched above her knees. Grant's eyes narrowed. Was that a flash of black lace, or was it his imagination?

"I wasn't born yesterday, Mr. Landon. We both know what the 'fine art of negotiating' really means. Her eyes met his. "Get as much as you can, while you can. Isn't that right?"

Were they still discussing the intricacies of contract negotiations? Or had they moved on to an entirely different sort of negotiation?

"Perhaps." Grant smiled. "But I've never taken pleasure in an arrangement that wasn't mutually agreeable."

Alicia Madigan gave a throaty laugh. "So I've heard." Her long legs scissored again. There was no mistaking the flash of black lace this time. "You know," she said softly, "I was as excited at the prospect as I was wary of the consequences of dealing with the famous Grant Landon."

Grant's smile tilted. "I have difficulty envisioning you as wary of anyone, Miss Madigan."

"Alicia, please. Surely, we don't have to be so formal now." The tip of her pale pink tongue peeked from between her teeth and slicked across her bottom lip as she rose from her chair. "In fact, I was thinking we might have a drink together. Perhaps dinner. And then—well, who knows?"

Grant felt his body tighten as she came toward him. He looked her over slowly, his hazel eyes moving the length of her body in frank appraisal. Instinct told him that he could take her now, that she *wanted* to be taken now. All he had to do was go to her, put his hands under that seemingly demure skirt, shove it above her thighs...

"You're very direct," he said, his voice a little thick as he pushed back his chair and got to his feet.

"I am." She put her hand on his arm; he could feel the heat of her fingers through the soft wool of his jacket. "Does it offend you?"

"On the contrary. I find it admirable." He lifted his hand to her cheek and stroked his forefinger across the prominent arch. "I'm a believer in honesty in relationships."

"So I've heard." She smiled. "It's a trait I admire."

Grant smiled, too. "But I should warn you that I am old-fashioned about some things."

"You're not going to tell me that it would be a conflict of interest for us to cultivate our friendship, are you?" Alicia Madigan said with a little laugh.

Slowly, his eyes never leaving hers, Grant reached out and cupped his hand lightly over her breast. He heard her catch her breath, the sound loud as a gunshot in the silence.

"Actually," he said, his tone almost conversational, "I was thinking about the concept of giving and taking." She gave a choked moan of pleasure as his thumb swept lightly across her breast; he felt the swift hardening of her nipple beneath her suit jacket. "And you ought to know that I prefer to be the one who decides what to give." His thumb moved again. "And what to take. Is that a problem?"

"Oh no," she said. He could see her fighting for control of herself. "No, that's not a problem at all. You can—"

His hand moved. Her fingers clamped tightly around his wrist as he stroked her; he could feel the sudden fierce tremor of excitement that swept through her body.

The realization that he'd so quickly cut through her cool, assertive exterior was almost as pleasing as it was disappointing. What she promised now didn't matter. Later, she would want something more, something he could not give.

There had been women who'd accused him of having no heart, but it wasn't true. He could take pleasure in a relationship—but love? Love was a word invented by greeting-card makers. It was not real. Any sensible man knew that, and Grant had always been a sensible man.

Suddenly, he felt weary, far older than his thirty-two years, and tired of this game he had played so many times before. He stepped back, took Alicia Madigan gently by the shoulders, and smiled at her.

"Give me your number," he said. "I'll call you."

"But..." Her blue eyes clouded. "I thought—"

"Not tonight," he said gently. "But soon. I promise."

There was a moment's silence, and then a tight smile curled across her mouth.

"I suppose I should be insulted—but I think I'd rather consider it a challenge." She bent and picked up her briefcase. "My number's in the book," she said. Her voice was cool, and gave no hint of what had just happened. "Please have the contract changes in my office first thing Monday morning."

Grant nodded, smiled, and watched as she made the long walk to the door. Once it shut after her, he blew out his breath.

"Hell," he muttered, as his gaze swept across the clock on his desk. He was running late. By the time he shaved, showered, then dressed, his date would be here. Kimberly would not like having to cool her heels, he thought as he took off his jacket and laid it neatly over the back of his desk chair.

But she'd wait.

They always did.

Crista Adams was running late, too, and she felt terrible about it—especially since she'd promised Danny she'd be on time tonight.

She paused to catch her breath on the fifth-floor landing of the Greenwich Village tenement. At least she'd remembered to stop for a bottle of wine. As for being late—well, that hadn't been her choice. Gus had asked her to stay an extra hour to fill in for one of the other girls and she'd ended up with a tableful of beer guzzlers who thought waitresses had been put on this planet for their amusement.

Crista grimaced as she headed toward her apartment. It wasn't worth thinking about. Getting hit on went with the territory down here, especially when Gus insisted that his waitresses wear short leather skirts, knee-high boots, and T-shirts that clung like a second skin. But the tips were good, you could work just about as many hours as you could handle and, slowly but steadily, she was beginning to save money toward the future.

Some day, she thought as she dredged out her keys, she'd have enough to open a little shop where she could sell the silver jewelry she loved to create. Until then, this life wasn't so bad. At least she was answerable to no one but herself. And if the loud-mouths and wise guys got the wrong idea about her and tried to push the issue... Crista smiled as she unlocked the apartment door. Well, she had her own security system just inside.

What fool would try any funny stuff, once he saw Danny?

"It's me," she called as she stepped into the postage-stamp-size living room. A gray cat with a mangled ear came hurrying toward her, meowing plaintively. Crista smiled and bent to pat its head. "Hello, Sweetness," she cooed. "Did you miss me?"

The cat wove through her ankles as she walked to the kitchen where a pot simmered on the old-fashioned gas stove, a delicious aroma of garlic floating into the air. She put down the wine, scooped the mane of silky black hair away from her high-cheekboned face, and leaned down for a look.

"Mmm," she sighed.

Danny's sauce was always wonderful. Crista grinned as she shrugged off her jacket and tossed it across a chair. What more could a woman ask of the person who shared her apartment? Danny could cook, he loved animals, he didn't mind the fact that she spent her spare time fashioning jewelry out of silver and beads—and he had more muscles than Sylvester Stallone.

That was the first thing she'd noticed about him, the day he'd shown up in answer to her ad—the day she'd been determined to turn him away.

"I want a female roommate," she'd said firmly. "My ad specifically said—"

"The ad says two bedrooms, doesn't it, Ms. Adams?"

"Yes, but—"

The gray cat had chosen that moment to come strutting in.

"Hey," Danny had said, "you've got a cat." He'd shot her a grin as he squatted down beside Sweetness. "I love cats."

Crista's smile had been politely dismissive. "That's very nice, Mr. Amato. But my ad distinctly said 'Single female to share 2 bedroom Village walk-up—'"

"Nice earrings. Never saw anything like 'em before."

She'd touched one of the little clusters of silver bells hanging from her lobes and then she'd frowned.

"Thank you. But—"

"Listen, Ms. Adams. I know what you're thinking."

Crista's violet eyes had been cool. "I doubt it."

"You're thinking," he'd said pleasantly, "this guy moves in here, he's gonna hit on me."

Crista hadn't flinched. "And won't you?"

"Tell me the truth, Ms. Adams. Am I your type?"

He wasn't. Oh, he was handsome, but the fact was that Crista had yet to meet a man who *was* her type—but that was nobody's business but her own.

"No," she'd said bluntly, "you're not."

"And you're not mine, Ms. Adams. You're certainly a looker, but the vibes are all wrong—if you know what I mean."

Crista had hesitated. Every loony in New York seemed to have answered her ad. This guy, at least, wasn't mumbling about trips back home to Mars. He'd already shown her his references—and, she'd suddenly realized, sharing an apartment with a man who looked like Mr. Muscle might turn out to be an unexpected bonus.

To her surprise and his, Crista had agreed to a week's trial—and she'd never regretted it, she thought as she filled a pot with water and set it on to boil. If Danny had one failing, it was that he was sometimes behind on his half of the rent payments, but struggling actors were not known for their wealth.

Anyway, there were more important things than money. Crista's smile dimmed. She knew that better than anyone. She'd spent her teen years in the lap of luxury, the ward of a coldhearted uncle she'd never known existed until her parents' deaths. Simon had wasted no time in telling her how her mother had lured her father from the bosom of his family.

"And you," he'd snapped, "are her very image, in looks and in temperament."

He had spent the next years determinedly trying to remake that image through private schooling and cultural tours of Europe. Shortly before Crista's twentieth birthday, the situation had become intolerable. She'd moved out, and Simon had washed his hands of her.

That had been months ago. Still, when she'd read of his death in the paper a few weeks before, she'd gone to his funeral. Simon would have laughed; he'd have called her sentimental, a vulgar emotion he'd abhorred. But he was all the family she had, and sometimes, in the darkest moments of the night, she thought about how alone she was...

"Hey." She looked up. Danny was standing in the doorway, his hair damp from the shower. "Why the long face?"

Crista cleared her throat. "What long face?" she said briskly.

"Did you hear the one about the camel and the goat?"

She groaned. "Only a thousand times."

"I've got a new version, guaranteed to make you smile."

He was right; the joke did make her smile. In fact, she almost forgot the brief sense of despair that had engulfed her moments ago...

Almost. But not quite.

Grant stood on the terrace of his Fifth Avenue penthouse, sipping a glass of Dom Pérignon from a Baccarat flute, waiting for Kimberly to reappear.

"Such a glum expression," she'd said in a little-girl voice, just before she'd traipsed off to the powder room. "Don't worry, darling. When I come back, I'll make you smile."

He doubted that, Grant thought grimly. He was bored, he was tired of watching Kimberly watch herself in every reflective surface, and he was hungry. What had his housekeeper left in the kitchen? *Canard a l'Orange*? Whatever it was, it had to wait until Kimberly put in an appearance.

He shot another look through the open terrace doors into the elegant white-on-white living room. Where the devil was she? She'd said she needed to fix her face—although what you could fix on that face was beyond him. It was so perfect it was almost expressionless, something he'd never noticed before tonight.

"Hell," Grant muttered, and put the champagne flute down none too gently on a glass-topped table.

What was wrong with him? The feeling of disquiet that had begun late this afternoon had grown so that now he felt edgy and irritable. A premonition, his sister, Kyra, would have said.

He frowned. Kyra? What did she have to do with anything? Why was he thinking of her when—

The telephone on the table beside him shrilled. He picked it up.

"Yes?" he said brusquely. It was Jane, his secretary.

A shape materialized at the far end of the living room. Kimberly was sauntering toward him, her hips swinging as if she were on a modeling runway. She was wearing a scarlet teddy, a sultry pout, and nothing else.

Grant's breath caught, but not because of Kimberly. He turned away and pressed the phone more tightly to his ear.

"I see. Thank you, Jane. You did the right thing. I can make it. Would you phone my sister and tell her I'm on my way? And my brothers. You have Zach's Boston number. Cade is in the Middle East. Ask Zach if— Fine. I'll be in touch."

He hung up the phone, cleared his throat, and turned to face Kimberly, who was breathing moistly against his neck.

"I'm sorry," he said, "but something's come up."

She giggled and put her hand on him. The scent of her perfume, sweet and cloying, filled his nostrils.

"Not yet it hasn't," she purred. "But it will."

Grant's hand clamped hard around her wrist. "I have a plane to catch," he said. "Take your time dressing. The doorman will put you in a taxi when you come down."

"A plane?" Kimberly said, her voice filled with bewilderment. "But I thought we..." Her voice rose as he brushed past her. "Grant, what's so important that...?"

He wondered what she would say if he told her what was so important, if he said, well, Kimberly, if you must know, my father—a man I feel less for than I would for a stranger—my father, Charles Landon, is dead.

But he only turned and strode through the perfect living room, up the curved staircase to his bedroom. By the time he came down again, carrying a leather weekend bag, he had forgotten Kimberly existed.

In the taxi to the airport he puzzled, briefly, over the sense of disquiet that had plagued him all day. He wasn't about to give any credence to the idea of premonitions. Still ...

Grant sighed wearily, sat back and closed his eyes.

In Greenwich Village, Crista paused with a forkful of pasta halfway to her lips.

"What's the matter?" Danny asked.

"I don't know," she said. "Just—just a funny feeling ..."

"A goose walked over your grave." He grinned at the look on her face. "Listen, when you have a grandmother from the Old Country, you pick up all kinds of weird stuff."

"A goose, huh?" Crista laughed, stabbed her fork into her spaghetti, and began to eat her dinner.

CHAPTER ONE

THE sun was coming up fast over the Rocky Mountains, but the highest peaks were still shrouded in mist and the wind blowing across Emerald Lake was chill. Grant, who'd worked up a sweat during his five-mile run, shivered a little as he entered the aspen grove that led to the Landon mansion.

Gravel crunched under his Nikes, the sound a gritty counterpoint to the rasp of his own breath. He'd run this distance every morning for almost as long as he could remember, but it was a long time since he'd done his running at this altitude. His hard muscles ached, his heart was pounding, his lungs were working hard...

And he was loving every minute of it.

How could he have forgotten how peaceful it was here? Except for a pair of startled mule deer, Grant had the lake and the slopes all to himself. No cars, no trucks, no people, nothing but the deer, the sky, and the mountains.

Damn, but this was one hell of a beautiful spot.

Grant's mouth twisted in a grimace. Except for the mansion rising just ahead, it was perfect.

The house was monstrous in size and in pretension. It should have been made of fieldstone and glass, with soaring, clean lines. Instead, it was massive, built of concrete and brick, and as out of place as it was opulent. The mansion didn't harmonize with its setting, it competed with it—and lost, Grant thought as he slowed to a walk. Hell, it was no contest.

His lips twisted again. "Be it ever so humble," he muttered as he trotted up the steps to the flagstone terrace, "there's no place like home."

He smiled bitterly as he snatched his towel from the lounge chair. If there was one thing this place had never been, it was a home. He'd hated the house when he was a boy and he hated it still.

It was a damned good thing he was leaving today. A week in this place was about all he could manage and still remain sane.

Grant wiped his face with the towel. He hadn't shaved since yesterday and the stubble of his dark beard rasped across the soft cotton. Tossing the towel aside, he reached for the Columbia Law School sweatshirt that lay on the chair, and yanked it down over his head. With a sigh, he raked his hair back from his forehead, turned and walked slowly across the terrace, and stood looking out at Emerald Lake, glittering like the jewel it had been named for under the first rays of the sun.

What a hell of a week this had been! He'd ended up having to install a private phone line, just so he could keep in touch with his New York office. The mansion's own lines, all eight of them, had been jammed with incoming calls and faxes from newspapers and wire services and what seemed like every moneyman, politico, and bigwig industrialist from coast to coast.

"It's a goddamned circus," Zach had muttered one morning, after the three Landon brothers had spent a frantic hour fielding calls.

"Yeah," Cade had said with a thin-lipped smile, "and the old man would have loved it."

Grant shook his head as he leaned his arms on the stone wall that surrounded the terrace. Cade was right. The old man certainly would have loved it—the fuss, the media attention, the brouhaha the day of the funeral, when vans from the TV stations, the limos, and the mourners' cars had caused a massive traffic jam on the roads leading to the cemetery where Charles had been laid to rest—oh yeah, he'd have loved that most of all.

Grant had hated every minute of it. Hell, he'd almost come to blows with a scum-sucking, freelance photographer who'd tried to slip inside the mausoleum to snag a shot of the old man's mahogany casket as it came to rest beside Ellen Landon's. Zach and Cade had damned near had to pull him off the guy.

Grant blew out his breath. That had been the only time he'd felt anything. First, rage at the intrusiveness of the photographer, and then a fierce stab of pain at the sight of his mother's casket, which was ridiculous. Not that Grant hadn't loved her—he had, of course. But Ellen had died years ago, when he was just a boy; his memories of her were dimmed by the passage of time, and besides, he was not the sort of man given to sentimentalizing the past.

His overreaction—obviously the result of exhaustion—must have shown in his face, because Kyra had slipped her hand in his and leaned into his shoulder.

"Hey," she'd whispered, "are you okay?"

Grant, feeling foolish, had nodded and squeezed her hand in reassurance.

"I'm fine," he'd whispered back. "What about you, Sis? How are you bearing up?"

Kyra had looked up. Her face was pale but, to his surprise, her eyes were clear and cool.

"Don't worry about me," she'd said. "I'm fine."

Afterward, the crowd of mourners had gathered at the mansion to offer condolences to Grant, Cade, Zach, and Kyra.

"It must be a comfort to you," old Judge Harris had said, his jowls quivering with solemnity, "to see how many of Denver's finest citizens have come to pay their last respects to your dear father."

"What he means," Zach had murmured as soon as the judge was out of earshot, "is that Denver's finest citizens have come to size up the new Landon regime."

Cade had grinned. "What he *really* means," he'd said, "is that they've decided to waste no time kissing ass."

His kid brother had been right, Grant thought as he straightened up and turned his back to the lake. Crossing the terrace, he snatched up his towel again and made his way through the French doors that opened into the library.

It was cool inside, almost cold; the heavy red leather chairs, massive oak tables, and book-lined walls looked particularly ugly in the pale morning light. Everything was silent. The only hint of life was in the rich aroma of freshly brewed coffee that drifted in the air.

Grant smiled tightly to himself as he made his way across the Aubusson carpet. If his father could see him now, the old man would frown and tell him that he was to use the back door in the future, when he came in all sweated up from something so stupid as running. And then his lip would curl with disdain at the sight of the sweatshirt and he'd launch into the speech he always made about fancy-pants schools, when what he really meant was that it enraged him that his eldest son had chosen to defy him.

A plump figure suddenly stepped out in front of him. Stella, who'd been the Landon housekeeper for as long as Grant could remember, gasped and pressed her hand to her ample bosom.

"My goodness, Mr. Grant, you did give me a start!"

"Good morning, Stella." Grant smiled. "I was just on my way to the kitchen. That coffee smells wonderful."

"Why didn't you let me know you were up? I'd have been down sooner, made you a proper breakfast. You go in the dinin' room and sit down while I make you somethin' to tide you over until the others come down."

Grant had a swift vision of the gargantuan breakfasts still laid out on the sideboard every morning, despite the fact that neither he, his brothers, nor Kyra ever put a dent in them.

"No," he said quickly, "thank you very much, Stella, but I'm afraid I haven't the time. I've an appointment in—" he frowned at his watch "—in less than an hour. But I will take a cup of coffee upstairs with me." He smiled and looped his arm lightly over her shoulders. "Did I ever tell you that you make the best coffee in the entire world?"

Color bloomed in her cheeks. "Go on," she said, but she smiled. "You just wait here, Mr. Grant, and I'll get you some."

"Don't be silly." Grant began walking slowly down the hall. "I know how to find the kitchen."

"Yes, but it's not right. Your father says—"

"My father's not master of this house anymore." He knew he'd spoken more sharply than he'd intended, and he softened the words with a quick smile. "Tell you what. I'll walk you to the kitchen and we'll get that cup of coffee together."

How long would it take everybody to get used to the change? he wondered moments later as he set his mug of coffee on the nightstand in his old bedroom.

Charles Landon wasn't master here anymore. The old man wasn't master of anything, he thought as he stripped off his shorts and shirt. The grim proof of that lay in what had happened yesterday, after the formal reading of the will.

Nothing in it had been a surprise. Charles had left his private fortune to Kyra, along with the house and its enormous land holdings, and he had left Landon Enterprises, the vast, multimillion-dollar conglomerate he had built, to his three sons.

The sun, streaming through the windows, felt good on Grant's naked body. He stretched his arms, flexing the muscles that bunched beneath his taut, tanned skin. Purposefully, he made his way into his private bathroom and turned the shower on to full.

The old man would have exploded if he'd seen what had happened once the reading of the will had ended. The lawyers had barely been out the door before Zach had spoken.

"Man, what a gift," he'd said sarcastically. "Just what I've always wanted—a piece of Landon Enterprises."

Cade had wasted no time. "I'll pass," he'd said. "You guys can keep my share."

Grant had bared his teeth in what he'd hoped was a smile. "Hell," he'd said, "don't be so generous, pal!" He'd gone to the cherry-wood bar, uncapped a bottle of Jack Daniel's bourbon, poured generous shots into heavy Waterford tumblers and said what he'd always known in his heart. "I'd steal hubcaps for a living before I had anything to do with Landon Enterprises."

Zach and Cade had both laughed, and Zach had raised his glass of bourbon high in the air.

"Okay," he'd said, "it's unanimous. The new directors of Landon Enterprises met and made their first, last, and only decision."

"Yeah," Grant had said, as the three tumblers clinked against each other. "By unanimous vote, the directors agreed to divest themselves of the company."

Within minutes, they'd agreed to put Landon's on the market and give the proceeds to charity. Then they'd raised their glasses again, this time in bittersweet celebration of finally admitting what they'd all always known.

Charles Landon's sons had, over the years, ignored their father, argued with him, feared him and despised him—but they had never loved him.

Grant stepped from the shower, toweled himself dry, then strolled naked into the bedroom. And so it was all over. Within hours, he'd be in New York, Zach would be in Boston, and Cade would be in London. Kyra, of course, would remain here, where she belonged and where she was happy.

Hell, he couldn't wait to get back to his own world, and his own life. There were the loose ends of that contract to tie up—and there were other loose ends, too. He smiled a little as he drew his shirt over his broad shoulders. He'd certainly been abrupt with Kimberly—Kimberly and that red teddy. But he'd been abrupt with women before, when the demands of the law had gotten in the way of his private life. A couple of dozen long-stemmed red roses, a box of Godiva chocolates . . .

Grant's smile tilted. Kimberly would come around.

And then there was the Madigan woman and that tantalizing glimpse of black lace she'd flashed each time she'd crossed those long legs.

He grinned as he stepped into his trousers. What a dilemma, to have to choose between the two—or not to choose. There were lots of women in New York. Beautiful women. A man could spend his life sipping nectar from all those sweet flowers. Not that he didn't believe in fidelity.

Grant looped his tie under his collar and knotted it. He was always faithful, he thought, smiling again—for as long as an affair lasted.

He looked into the mirror as he put on his jacket. The runner in shorts and sweatshirt was gone, replaced by a meticulously groomed man in a Savile Row suit, but then, that was who he was. The man who'd come into this bedroom with an unshaven face, grungy shorts, and a sweatshirt was just a leftover from a life he'd long ago put behind him.

Why he even kept his old running clothes was beyond him; they were so beat up that they should have been tossed out years ago.

With a grimace, Grant stuffed the shirt and shorts into a pocket of his weekend bag. This was not the time for philosophical musings. He had an ap-

pointment to keep—a breakfast meeting requested by
Victor Bayliss, who'd been Charles's number one yes-
man.

"You meet with the guy," his brothers had said with
unseemly haste. "It takes a lawyer to talk to a lawyer."

Heartless bastards, Grant thought with a fond smile
as he closed the bedroom door after him. Not that he
minded. Bayliss undoubtedly wanted this meeting so
he could cozy up to the new Landon management.

Grant could hardly wait to see the man's face when
he heard the news.

A couple of hours later, Grant threw open the massive
front door to the Landon mansion, slammed it shut
behind him, and strode down the hall to the dining
room. They were all gathered there, just as he'd expected. Cade and Zach were horsing around as if they
hadn't a care in the world while a smiling Kyra looked
on.

Hell, Grant thought angrily, why did he have to be
the one to drop the bombshell?

"Dammit," he snapped, "what's going on here?
We're not kids anymore, in case you've forgotten."

Cade and Zach swung toward him, their faces reg-
istering surprise.

"Grant?" Kyra said. "Are you okay?"

He dropped the manila folder filled with bad news
on the table, walked to the sideboard, and poured
himself a cup of coffee.

"I'm fine," he said, but he knew, from the looks
on their faces, that he wasn't fooling anybody.

"So?" Cade asked after a minute. "What did
Bayliss want to talk about?"

A muscle knotted in Grant's jaw. "Trouble," he said grimly. "That's what he wanted to talk about."

Zach frowned. "What kind of trouble?"

Grant picked up the file folder. There was no point in beating around the bush; this would have to be dealt with quickly.

"See for yourselves," he said. He pulled papers from the folder and handed one stack to Cade, the other to Zach. Kyra looked at him, her brows raised, and he smiled reassuringly. There was nothing here to worry his little sister, thank goodness. After a moment, she turned toward the window.

Cade was the first to react.

"According to this report," he said, looking at Grant, "this Dallas oil company Landon owns— Gordon's, it's called—is going to go under any minute."

"What oil company?" Zach said, his expression puzzled. "I just read a profile on a Landon acquisition called Triad. It's some kind of Hollywood production outfit—and it's gonna sink like a stone."

Grant nodded grimly. "You're both right. Landon bought both firms to bail them out. Instead, we seem to have helped them get into worse condition."

Cade bristled. "What's this 'we' stuff, big brother?"

"Are you forgetting, Cade?" Grant swung toward him. "It's us, as of yesterday. Like it or not, we're Landon Enterprises. And we will be, until we find a buyer."

Neither Zach nor Cade needed to be force-fed reality. Grant saw the understanding dawn in both their faces.

If either Gordon Oil or Triad Productions went under, selling Landon would become a nightmare. The company would have a hole in its balance sheet large enough to sink a battleship. Only a fool would buy it then.

Grant's jaw clenched. His hand went to his pocket, where a scrap of paper lay. The paper was yet another problem, one so ridiculous he couldn't bring himself to mention it. Not now anyway; not until they'd figured a way out of this mess.

"Tell Bayliss to deal with this," Cade said.

"Bayliss retired as of this morning. He said he was too old to face another Colorado winter." Grant smiled tightly. "Seems we read him wrong. He's going to spend the rest of his days in the Virgin Islands, sipping piña coladas."

"Goodwin, then. Bayliss's second in command. He can—"

"Goodwin's got a dozen things on his plate already."

"Then what—"

"Oh, for heaven's sake!" The brothers swung around. Kyra was glowering at them with a look on her face that said all three of them were fools. "What's with you guys? Are you stupid, or what? A ten-year-old could figure this out!" She turned an angry glare on Zach. "You're the financial whiz, aren't you? Surely you could fly out to the coast, take a look at Triad's books, and decide what can be done to help it."

"Me? Don't be silly. I've got people waiting for me in Boston. I can't just—"

"And you," she snapped at Cade. "You're the genius who knows all about oil. And here's this little company having a problem." She slapped her hands onto her hips. "Would it be too much to hope that maybe you might be the one to check things out in Dallas?"

"It's out of the question! I've business in London. I can't—"

"She's right," Grant said brusquely. "You guys could get a handle on things faster than anybody else."

There was a moment's silence. Cade and Zach looked at each other, and then Zach threw up his arms in defeat.

"Two days," he said, "and not a second more."

Cade nodded. "Okay. Two days, and then . . . Wait just a minute." He swung toward Grant. "What about you? Don't tell me you're the only one of us who gets to walk away from this mess?"

Grant's hand clamped tightly around the paper in his pocket. Cade was flying to Texas to find out why an oil company was going under; Zach was heading for California to get a handle on a film outfit. And he—he was going back to New York to—to—

Jesus. It was ridiculous, but he was stuck with it. He took a deep breath.

"I've got my own mess to deal with. It seems some old pal of Father's named him guardian of his twelve-year-old kid."

"And?"

"And," he said through his teeth, "until she turns twenty-one, I seem to have inherited her."

He saw the smiles begin to curve across his brothers' faces, saw even Kyra try, and fail, to maintain a neutral expression. But what choice was there? He was an attorney, he lived and practiced in New York. The girl lived there, too—it was no contest, he thought grimly. The child was his burden by default.

His brothers were looking at each other, their smiles rapidly becoming grins, and he glowered at them.

"You guys think this is funny? Listen, we can always swap jobs. I'll take on Hollywood, or Dallas, and one of you can—"

"No," Zach said quickly, "no, that's okay, old buddy. I'll deal with Hollywood, Cade'll handle Dallas." His lips twitched. "And I bet you're going to make one hell of a terrific baby-sitter."

Cade suppressed a snort of laughter. Grant swung toward him.

"This—this is not funny," he choked, and then, suddenly, the grim look left his face and he burst out laughing. "Hell," he said, "I can't believe it, either."

Laughing, the three men moved into a tight circle, clapped each other on the back, then joined right hands as they had when they were kids.

"To the Deadeye Defenders," Cade said.

"To the Deadeyes," Grant echoed, and they grinned happily at each other.

Cade stepped back. "Time to get started."

Zach nodded. "Yeah. I'll see you guys before I leave."

They both hurried from the room. Grant was following after them when Kyra caught his sleeve. "Grant?"

He looked down at her and smiled. "Hey, princess, I almost forgot you were here!"

Kyra gave a short, sharp laugh. "Isn't that the truth!"

"Well, what is it, sweetheart?"

"I wonder..." She hesitated. "I was wondering how you feel about this place. Is it important to you?"

At first, the question puzzled him, but then he understood. Kyra was worried that her brothers might feel cheated because their father had left the mansion solely to her. Grant put his arm around her shoulders.

"This house will always be important to me," he said, "with you living in it."

"I don't mean that." Her tone was impatient. "This isn't about me, Grant, it's about you. And Cade. And Zach. I need to know if you care about the house, and the grounds, and—"

"I'm certain they feel as I do," Grant said in a kindly voice. "This place makes you happy, and your happiness is all that matters to us."

Kyra wrenched free of his arm. "Dammit," she said, her face flushed, "sometimes you all remind me of Father!"

Grant drew back. "What in hell is that supposed to mean?"

"It means—it means none of you listens. You hear what you want to hear, what you think you ought to hear, what—" Kyra blinked. "Sorry. I must be tired. It's been a long week." She smiled, reached up, and laid her hand against his chest. "I bet you'll be a fine guardian for this girl."

He frowned. "I'll do my duty, of course."

"But if she needs a friend..."

Grant laughed. "I am not about to be a 'friend' to this child. I will pay her bills, see to it that her future is secure—those are the responsibilities of a guardian."

Kyra sighed. "I suppose you're right." She stood on her toes and pressed her lips to his cheek. "I'm sorry I jumped on you a few minutes ago, Grant. I love you. I love all my brothers—and I always will.''

Grant hugged her. "And we love you, princess.'' He kissed her forehead, then made his way past her. When he reached his room, he closed the door and let out a long sigh.

Kyra was sweet and wonderful, and he'd have willingly given his life for her—but did she really think he'd play big brother to—what was her name? Crista, that was it. Crista Adams.

One of his law partners had a daughter Crista's age; from what Grant had seen, the poor guy was adrift in a sea of orthodontia, acne, and adolescent angst.

But he wouldn't face any of those problems. As Crista Adams's guardian, he'd simply be responsible for approving her expenses and signing the checks to meet them. Now that he thought about it—although he'd be damned if he'd ever admit as much to Cade and Zach—he was getting off easy.

Crista Adams's guardian, hmm? He zipped shut his weekend case, picked it up, and walked out of the room.

What could be simpler?

CHAPTER TWO

GRANT generally liked Mondays. They put a clean start to the week ahead, but somehow this one already had the feel of disaster.

Why wouldn't it? he thought, glaring at himself in the bathroom mirror as he shaved. He was about to meet the child who had become his unwanted responsibility, like it or not.

What had seemed a minor inconvenience last week in Denver was looking more and more like a catastrophe waiting to happen. A little judicious checking of guardianship laws suggested that he'd have to do more than sign checks. He might have to offer advice. Even guidance.

Grant's mouth thinned as he rinsed off his razor. What he knew about children could fit in a pea pod with room left over. And he didn't know a damned thing about Crista Adams.

He had phoned Simon Adams's attorney right away but Horace Blackburn was out of the country, his holiday guarded with almost religious fervor by an iron-willed secretary who'd agreed to set up this meeting on her boss's first day back only after Grant's growing exasperation had become evident.

But she'd steadfastly refused to release the Adams file so that he could, at least, familiarize himself with the simple details of his ward's life.

Grant splashed some cologne on his face and strode from the bathroom. Was the child living in her

31

uncle's house with a governess or was she away at boarding school? Was she a snot-nosed brat or a well-behaved young lady? Had she been traumatized by the loss of her uncle?

Did she expect her new guardian to take her uncle's place?

Jaw set, Grant undid the towel knotted at his hips and tossed it aside. The child would simply have to realize that her entire situation had changed, and if she couldn't cope with that change, she'd be in for a rough ride.

At eight-thirty, just as he was about to leave, the telephone rang. It was his driver, calling to tell him that his car had a flat.

"No problem," Grant said. "I can grab a taxi."

But it had started to rain. Finding a cab was impossible at rush hour on a rainy Monday. With a muttered curse, Grant gave it up and sprinted for the nearest subway station.

The platform was crowded and he paced its length with growing irritation. When a train finally came shrieking into the station, the crowd surged forward as if it were the last train anyone would ever see. Grant set his jaw and shouldered his way inside.

By the time he emerged on Wall Street, his mood had gone from bad to grim. Finding that he had at least another three blocks to go in the rain without an umbrella did not improve it.

"Dammit," he snarled to no one in particular. He turned up the collar of his jacket, ducked his head against the rain, and hurried down the street.

Crista was walking as fast as she could toward the building that housed Blackburn, Blackburn, and Katz but it wasn't easy when the ridiculously high heels on her boots kept slipping on the slick pavement.

She sighed, thinking how much better she'd feel if she were wearing her own clothes to this meeting. But the meeting was at nine, and she had to be back in the Village to start work by eleven. There wasn't any choice, except to wear this silly getup under her raincoat.

The letter from her uncle's attorney had arrived by registered mail on Saturday.

Dear Miss Adams,
Your presence is required at this office Monday morning promptly at nine regarding the provisions of your late uncle's will.

It was signed by Horace Blackburn, LL.B., J.D.

Crista had frowned. What was this about provisions in Uncle Simon's will? There wouldn't be anything in the will that concerned her. Simon had made that clear when she'd moved out of his home.

"You will not get one penny from me, young woman," he'd said shrilly, wagging a bony finger in her direction. "I'm going to cut you off without a cent!"

"I never wanted anything from you, Uncle," she'd responded—nothing he'd wanted to give her, at any rate.

So what could the estimable Horace Blackburn, LL.B., J.D., be talking about? Did some kind of legal mumbo jumbo require him to inform her that Simon had written her out of his will?

Well, she'd thought as she dialed Blackburn's office, he could just tell her that over the phone.

A recorded voice had informed her that the offices were closed until Monday morning at nine.

Crista had grimaced. She'd just have to wait until then to make the call....

Maybe it was impulsiveness. Maybe it was stubborn pride and the determination not to be intimidated by anyone, traits that had always infuriated her uncle. But sometime between Saturday afternoon and Sunday evening, she'd changed her mind.

Crista had decided to keep the appointment.

She'd met Horace Blackburn once when Simon had consulted him about transferring her from one boarding school to another. A prissy man with the same icy bearing as his client, Blackburn's disapproval of her had been written all over his face.

Wouldn't it be wonderful to smile sweetly at him and tell him where to get off after he'd read the words he undoubtedly hoped would bring tears to her eyes?

The more she'd thought about it, the more she'd looked forward to the chance.

But reality wasn't measuring up to the fantasy, Crista thought glumly as she turned down Canal Street. Things had gone wrong from the minute she'd awakened this morning. She'd slept through the first jangling call of her alarm clock, and then the gray cat had managed to get himself stuck behind the refrigerator. By the time she'd finally dashed from the apartment, Crista had been running late.

The bus had pulled out just as she'd reached the stop, and neither frantic shouting or jumping up and down had slowed it down or brought it back. So she'd caught the crosstown instead, intending to transfer to a downtown bus at Broadway, but somehow she'd miscalculated.

Now she was walking the last four long blocks in the rain, wondering why on earth she'd ever thought a face-to-face confrontation with Horace Blackburn would be a good idea.

She hunched deeper into the collar of her raincoat. The wind was picking up now, driving the rain before it. Her hair would be as tangled as a bird's nest by the time she reached Blackburn's office, and whatever rain-defeating abilities her thin coat once had were long gone. She didn't even want to think about what the dampness seeping through it might be doing to her already snug T-shirt.

Crista sighed as she stepped off the curb. She'd have been better off sticking to Plan A, she thought as she hurried across the intersection. She could have phoned Blackburn this morning and told him, in her best lockjawed, boarding-school accent, that she didn't give a fig for whatever it was he had to tell her, that he could either make his little speech over the phone or he could—

"Look out!"

The warning came too late. Crista's head came up just as the man barreled into her. Her right foot, already up on the curb, slid out from under her. She gave an outraged cry, windmilled her arms in a desperate attempt to keep her boots from bidding a fast farewell to the pavement, and went stumbling backward into the street just as a truck, horn blaring, came racing into the intersection.

The man's arms swept around her. "I've got you," he said, swinging Crista off her feet and onto the pavement as the truck thundered past, drenching them both in a spray of water.

They stood looking at each other in shocked silence and then Crista let out a long, shaky breath.

"Ohmygod," she whispered as she clung to the hard, broad shoulders of her rescuer.

"Oh my God?" Her rescuer's voice was deep and harsh and very angry. "Oh my God? Is that all you can say after you almost killed us both?"

Crista blinked. His face, as harsh and as angry as his voice, was inches from hers; his eyes—some strange combination of blue and brown and green—were cold with fury.

"Me?" she said. Her head lifted. "Me?" she repeated, her voice shooting up the scale in indignation. "*I* almost killed us both?" She glared back at him, shoved her drenched hair back from her eyes, and twisted free of his grasp. "You ran into me, remember?"

"Where are you from, lady? Didn't anybody tell you that you're supposed to watch where you're going in the big city?"

"I *was* watching where I was going," Crista said in her best New York fashion. "You were the one who was tearing along like a linebacker for the Jets."

The man's eyes grew flinty. "Thank you for the apology. And now, if you don't mind, I'd like to get by."

"That makes two of us," Crista said, her tone as nasty as his.

She stepped to her right. The man stepped to his left. They glared at each other, then made the same moves in reverse. He shook his head, muttered something, then made a mock-chivalrous sweeping gesture with his arm.

"Ladies first," he said, his tone heavy with sarcasm.

Crista sniffed. "Try keeping that in mind. It might save another woman from almost getting knocked down."

It was, she thought, a fair exit line—but as she started past him, her right ankle buckled. With a cry of alarm, she stumbled—and was caught in the man's arms again.

"What now?" he demanded.

Crista's brows drew together. "I don't know," she said. "I was fine until I put weight on my foot. But when I did, it just—"

"Hell, I get it." She gasped as his hands dug into her forearms. "What comes next? An ambulance ride to the nearest emergency room, where you suddenly develop an incurable headache and back pains?"

"What are you talking about? I never said—"

"I warn you, you're wasting your time trying a scam like this on me. I'm an attorney, and—"

"An attorney!" Crista twisted away from him and slapped her hands on her hips. "Of course," she said, her lip curling, "I might have known."

"Spoils your little scheme, doesn't it?" Grant smiled tightly. "Trust me, madam. There's nothing you can try that I haven't seen before."

No, he thought, with a catch of his breath, no, he had not seen a face like hers before.

Her eyes were enormous, the color of violets. Her mouth was rosy and heart-shaped, centered between a small, slender nose and a feminine, yet determined, chin. Clusters of tiny silver bells swayed from a pair of delicate ears that were framed by a silky tumble of ebony hair in which raindrops glistened like tiny jewels.

For a man who had seen everything, Grant was suddenly speechless.

"What's the matter?"

Grant blinked. She was eyeing him narrowly, her face tilted at a questioning angle. The anger was still there but something else was there, too. Wariness? Suspicion?

He sighed. Hell, she was right to look at him like that. Only a nut—or a man in a very bad mood—would go off the deep end the way he had.

She'd run into him, or he'd run into her—who could tell? And what did it matter? The one indisputable fact was that their collision had been forceful. For all he knew, she damned well might have twisted her ankle when she fell back off the curb.

"Nothing's the matter," he said. "Look, I'm sorry I've been so—"

"Unpleasant?" That determined chin shot forward. "Hostile? How about just plain nasty?"

He tried a polite smile. "I was just heading into that building," he said, and nodded toward an entryway on his right. "Why don't we step inside the lobby? You can get off that foot and I'll check to see if—"

Her hand drove into his belly, hard enough to make the breath shoot from his lungs.

"That's the most pathetic come-on I've ever heard," she snarled. "Next you're going to ask me to come up to your office so you can examine me on your couch."

"Don't be a fool. I simply meant—"

"Oh, I know exactly what you meant." Crista's chin lifted. "First you knock me down, then you accuse

me of faking an injury, and now you're trying to—
to—"

"Listen, lady—"

"I'm on my way to a meeting with my attorney this
very minute. I swear, I'll tell him to sue you for—
for—"

"The charge is stupidity, lady. First degree stupidity," Grant said coldly. "Go on, limp your way to
wherever it is you're going. And good luck to the next
poor chump you run into."

"The same to you," Crista said, and flounced past
him.

She didn't get very far. This time, she didn't so
much stumble as drop to her knees.

"Oh," she said in surprise.

"Give me a break," Grant said wearily, stooped,
and swung her up into his arms.

"Hey," she said, "what are you doing?"

Being a glutton for punishment, Grant thought as
he carried her toward the building where Horace
Blackburn's office was located. Hell, he thought
grimly, at least he was getting closer to that damned
meeting.

"You put me down!"

She was beating her fists against his shoulder, but
Grant ignored her. At some later point, he thought
with bemused detachment, he'd probably laugh at all
this, especially at how a woman who felt so soft and
smelled so good could land such solid, uncompro-
mising punches.

Right now, all he could hope was that none of the
passersby tossing amused smiles in his direction was
Horace Blackburn.

Grant shouldered open the lobby door and made for a marble planter that held a scrawny rubber tree trying to survive. With a grunt, he dumped his burden unceremoniously on the planter's edge.

"No couch," he said briskly as he knelt down before her. "But then, you can't have everything in this life, can you?"

"Let me alone," she snapped as he reached for her foot.

"I'm checking to see what you've done to yourself."

"What I've done? You've got to be kidding! You ran me over, you called me a swindler, you—you kidnapped me—"

"I told you," he said pleasantly as he grasped her ankle. "Sue me. But first you're going to have to take this boot off."

"Not on your life! Dammit, I didn't ask you to—" The furious words ground to a halt. "What's so funny?"

"You won't need an ambulance or an orthopedist." Grant looked up at her, his lips twitching. "What you will need is a shoe repair shop."

Crista frowned as she leaned forward. "What?"

"It's your heel. It broke when you—when we—collided. That's why you had trouble keeping your balance."

Crista shut her eyes as the man began to chuckle. But she couldn't blame him. What a fool she'd made of herself, starting the minute they'd bumped into each other and going straight through to that performance she'd put on as he carried her inside this lobby.

She was in a terrible mood, angry at herself and the world, but he had no way of knowing that. He was just a stranger and she'd let it all out on him.

She took a deep breath. "Look," she said, and opened her eyes....

The apology died on her lips. He was still holding her foot, but he wasn't smiling any longer. Instead, he was taking a slow, steady inventory, that topaz gaze of his sweeping up the length of her inch by inch.

Crista knew, with awful certainty, what he was seeing. The T-shirt. The ridiculous leather skirt. The stupid boots...

Those incredible boots, Grant thought. They were the sexiest things he'd ever seen. And that skirt—it was leather, like the boots, and it barely came to mid-thigh. Above it, a wide belt cinched an impossibly slender waist and above that...

Oh yes. Above that, her breasts rose in exquisite fullness, rounded and high and encased in a pale pink cotton shirt that had been dampened by the rain. He could see the outline of her nipples so clearly defined that the need to reach out and touch them, to stroke them until they hardened in need, was almost overpowering.

"Well?" Her voice was low pitched, controlled, and very cold. "Have you had a good look, little boy?" She pulled her foot free of his hand and, with a lurch, got to her feet. "Then run home to Mama and I'll be on my way."

Grant rose, too. Her eyes had gone from violet to plum. She was angry at him again, which was laughable—almost as laughable as her pretended outrage when she'd thought he was coming on to her a few minutes ago.

Why would a woman dress this way unless that was exactly what she wanted from every man she met?

"Of course," he said silkily. "I wouldn't want to keep you. An appointment with your—ah—your attorney, isn't that what you said?"

Crista drew her raincoat around her. "You go to hell," she said. With as much dignity as she could manage, considering the broken boot heel, she turned and walked toward the door.

Damn him, she thought, trying not to tremble. And damn herself even more for letting him do that to her. It was a long time since she'd cared how men looked at her in this awful outfit.

But this man, the arrogant bastard, had more than wanted her. He had judged her. Not that she was surprised. Even soaked to the skin, he wore his money and his breeding like a badge of office. People who didn't meet his hard-hearted standards, who didn't measure up to some rigid set of rules of his own making, were beneath his contempt.

He didn't even believe her story about having a meeting to attend. Well, for all she knew, she didn't. She was so late now that...

Crista stopped as the directory on the wall caught her eye. Blackburn, Blackburn, and Katz were located in this building, on the twentieth floor.

She spun around. There were two elevators, and the doors of both were just shutting. The man might be in either one.

So what?

"Hey," she yelled, "wait!"

The doors jerked, stopped, then slid open. Crista hurried into the car. There were two occupants. A middle-aged woman with a briefcase—and him.

Crista shot him a cold look, then turned and folded her arms across her breasts. The elevator climbed slowly. At the third floor, the doors opened. The woman with the briefcase stepped out, and the doors closed again.

Crista counted silently as the car moved upward again. At the sixth floor, it stopped. She turned and glared at the man, who was leaning back against the wall, his feet crossed at the ankles.

"Sorry," he said with a contemptuous smile. "I'm not getting out yet—but feel free to choose any floor you like."

Crista's jaw tightened. "Don't I wish I could!"

"Following me is pointless. I don't know what you want, but—"

"Don't flatter yourself, mister! I have as much right to be here as you do. I have—"

"An appointment. Sure."

Crista heard the disdain in his words. She told herself it didn't matter, that the opinion of this stranger meant less than nothing to her—but she was already swinging toward him.

"Has anybody ever told you what an absolutely vile human being you are?"

His eyes narrowed. "Listen, lady. You've pushed your luck about as far as it goes. If I were you—"

"You are the most—the most arrogant, insolent, coldhearted, unfeeling son of a bitch—"

She cried out as he grabbed her and drew her to him. Her hand flew toward the control panel but he slammed his fist against it first.

The car shuddered to a halt.

"Hell," he growled, "I've taken just about enough from you!"

Deep inside, Grant could hear a cold, rational voice warning him that he was going over the edge—but he wasn't listening. No woman who looked like this should blame a man for looking at her, for wanting her—for needing to silence her in the most primitive way.

Grant gave up the battle and plunged into a time when men fought saber-toothed tigers.

He pulled her into his arms, ignoring the beat of her fists against his chest, his mouth dropping to hers in a kiss that demanded not just repentance but submission.

Crista offered neither. When he lifted his head, she spat a name into his face that the voice inside him assured him he more than deserved.

Let her go, Grant told himself. Dammit, man, let her go.

But the darkness reached for him again.

His hands fisted in her hair and his mouth descended toward hers. Again, he kissed her, branding her with his anger. Again, she fought back.

Grant went still. What in hell was he doing? He was not a man who took without giving. He was not a man who wanted without being wanted in return. And, God, that was what he needed from this woman. He needed her to want him, to part her lips for his kiss, to reach out to hold him and turn to fire in his arms.

Slowly, he bent his head, brushed his mouth against hers in soft, gentle strokes. His hands shifted, his fingers threading into the spill of her hair so that her head was tilted back and she was captive to his kiss. He kissed her again and again, each kiss tender and sweet, until he felt the tension and the fear leaving her body, until he felt it being replaced by something else.

She made a little sound, one the tiny bells of her earrings seemed to echo. Grant felt her body soften, felt the sudden heat of her, and he whispered words of reassurance against her mouth.

Crista swayed forward. Her lips parted; she whimpered as his mouth slanted over hers, hungry now, and demanding. Slowly, she rose toward him, she lifted herself to him....

The car lurched to life and Grant and Crista fell away from each other. In the silence, Grant could hear nothing but the rasp of his own breathing, the dull droning of the elevator's motor, and then the sound of the car stopping and the doors opening.

He swallowed, his eyes on her face. "Listen," he said thickly, "listen—"

"You louse," she hissed, and she slapped him so hard across the face that his head rocked back.

When she lifted her hand a second time, he caught hold of her wrist.

"Don't," he said very softly. After a long moment, he let go of her, turned, and stepped from the car.

He moved down the corridor like an automaton, his eyes locked on the ornate door ahead that bore the name Blackburn, Blackburn, and Katz.

What in hell had just happened to him? He'd behaved like a Neanderthal. Jesus, he'd acted like a man who'd lost his mind.

At the door, he paused, took a breath, and wiped his hand across his mouth. Then he took another breath and pushed the door open.

The week in Denver, and the funeral, had obviously put him off stride much more than he'd realized. And now, he was supposed to take on a responsibility that he surely didn't want? To hell with that, he thought as he reached the reception desk.

Blackburn, Blackburn, and Katz were just going to have to find themselves a different baby-sitter for Crista Adams.

The receptionist smiled politely. "Good morning, sir."

"Good morning," Grant said. "My name is Landon, and I have an appointment with—"

"Excuse me."

He swore under his breath as the woman from the elevator maneuvered into the space next to him.

"Do yourself a favor," he said. "Don't make a bigger fool of yourself than you already have."

She didn't even look at him. "I have an appointment," she said to the receptionist.

Grant slapped his hand on the desk. "This is ridiculous! This woman hasn't—"

"It was for nine o'clock," she said, shooting Grant a look. "But I was detained."

The receptionist smiled uncomfortably. "And you are Miss . . . ?"

"Adams," the woman said, drawing herself up. "Crista Adams."

CHAPTER THREE

CRISTA sat in a straight-backed chair opposite Horace Blackburn's desk, doing her best to carry on a conversation.

Yes, she was well. No, it had been no trouble finding his office. Yes, it was a long time since they'd seen each other.

And all the time, she kept reminding herself that she hadn't come out in the pouring rain and broken the heel of her boot and made herself at least an hour late for work just for a round of polite chitchat.

She had come to show her uncle's attorney that the life she'd left behind didn't mean a damn to her—but how could she do that when all her energies were focused on the man standing a few feet away, the man whose eyes, she knew, had never left her...

The man who had done such an outstanding job of making her look and feel like a fool?

What was he doing here? Why was he part of this meeting with Blackburn?

Crista had asked for answers, but no one had offered any. She'd given her name to the receptionist, and the next thing she knew, all hell had broken loose.

The man beside her had turned so white she'd thought he was going to pass out.

"Who?" he'd said in a strangled voice. "Who?"

Crista had no idea why he'd looked so stunned or why he'd sounded like a demented owl, but his distress had been so wonderful to see that she'd taken a few seconds to enjoy it. Then she'd dredged up the tight-jawed boarding-school accent she'd intended to save for Horace Blackburn.

"I said, my name is Crista Adams—not that it's any of your business."

"Crista Adams," he'd muttered. His color had come flooding back in an alarming rush of crimson and he'd given a short, terrible bark of laughter. "She's Crista Adams," he'd said to the receptionist, who sat gaping at them. "Can you believe that?"

"Yes, sir," the woman had said, and she'd reached quickly for the telephone. "Why don't I call Mr. Blackburn? He's been expecting Miss Adams, and—"

"Yes." And suddenly all the laughter was done with. The man had leaned over the reception desk, his eyes flat and cold. "Why don't you do that? While you're at it, tell him Grant Landon is here. And tell him that if he wants to live through the rest of the day, he'd better get his butt out here pronto!"

The receptionist had shot a look at the telephone, thought better of it, then gone flying down the hall. Seconds later, Blackburn had come hurrying toward them.

"My dear Miss Adams," he'd purred. "And Mr. Landon. How nice to meet you, sir."

"Cut the crap, Blackburn," Grant Landon had snarled.

It had been wonderful, seeing it all—the arrogant bastard named Landon in a rage, Horace Blackburn in a panic—so wonderful that Crista had been willing to simply stand by and watch while Landon maneuvered the hapless attorney into the corner. After a few moments of a terse, inaudible conversation, Blackburn had led them both here, to his office.

By then, Crista had begun asking questions and demanding answers, but neither man had offered any.

Now, Landon stood lounging against the wall, his arms crossed over his chest, his feet crossed at the ankles. It was a casual, I-don't-give-a-damn posture— but it wasn't fooling Crista. The tension in him was almost palpable.

But why? Crista cast a cautious glance in his direction, her gaze flying over him, taking in the hard, handsome face with its blade of a nose, the firm mouth, the slightly cleft chin; her eyes drifted to the broad shoulders, lean body, and long legs.

Whoever and whatever this man was, she was certain he was accustomed to giving orders and having them obeyed. Standing around while a prissy little sycophant like Horace Blackburn droned on and on, his nose twitching like a rodent's, was surely not something Grant Landon did very often.

Then why was he doing it now? What did he have to do with Blackburn?

Better still, what did he have to do with her?

"...more comfortable, Miss Adams?"

Crista blinked and looked toward Blackburn, who was peering at her over the top of his reading glasses and smiling, if that was what you wanted to call that stiff baring of his yellow teeth. It was costing him plenty to be polite, and while that realization gave her pleasure, it also only added to the mystery.

Why should Horace Blackburn treat her with such deference? It just didn't make sense, but then nothing that had happened for the past hour made sense.

"Miss Adams? I asked if you wouldn't like to take your coat off. It must be wet and uncomfortable."

Grant Landon made a noise, something halfway between a laugh and a cough. Crista's face flamed but she didn't so much as glance in his direction.

"Thank you," she said, "but I'm fine."

"Are you sure? All this rain..."

"Mr. Blackburn." Crista cleared her throat. It was time to restore the balance of power. "Mr. Blackburn," she said more firmly, "I want to know what's going on here."

"Of course, my dear. I know you must have questions and I'll be happy to answer them—in good time. But first"

"I want them answered now," Crista said even more firmly. "Why did you ask me to come here?" She jerked her head in Grant's direction but her eyes remained locked on Blackburn's face. "And why is that man in the room?"

"Miss Adams—"

"What a good idea, Horace." Grant's voice fairly purred with malice. Crista swung toward him. His lips were curved in what she suspected was meant to be a smile, but the effect was anything but pleasant. "Why not tell Miss Adams what she wants to know?" He unfolded his arms, examined the fingernails of his right hand with great concentration, then offered Blackburn another smile. "I'm sure she'll be especially pleased when you explain my presence. In fact, I can hardly wait to hear her cries of joy."

Blackburn turned a furious shade of pink. "Mr. Landon, if you'd just bear with me—"

"No. No, Horace, I am not going to bear with you." Grant moved toward the desk and Blackburn shrank back into his chair. "I've done that, and look where it got me!"

"I realize some errors were made, but—"

"What kind of man goes on vacation without telling his secretary that she's to bring important matters to his attention immediately?"

"Mr. Landon. Grant, please—"

"If I'd been able to read the Adams file, at least today might not be quite the fiasco it's becoming. But—"

Crista's brow furrowed. "What Adams file? Is there a file about me? What's he talking about, Mr. Blackburn?"

"Mr. Landon," Blackburn said, "I have already apologized. If you would only—"

"But no. I could not get my hands on that damned file." Grant straightened up, shot Blackburn an angry glare, and stalked across the room. "Your secretary guarded it with all the zeal of a rottweiler. And now, as a result, this damned situation has the tranquillity of a mine field! Dammit, man!" Grant jabbed his finger in Crista's direction. "How in hell could you have permitted me to think that she was a twelve-year-old child?"

"Me?" Crista said, looking from one man to the other. "But—but that's ridiculous. Why would you have thought about me at all?"

Grant bared his teeth in a feral smile. "An excellent question, Miss Adams. But I think I'd prefer leaving it for Mr. Blackburn to answer."

"I want to know what's going on here," Crista said, rising from her chair. "Who are you talking about? Who thought I was a child?"

"Everyone," Grant said tightly. "My father. And my father's assistant." He looked at her. "And, of course, me."

Crista's eyebrows lifted. "Really," she said. Her violet eyes narrowed. "Well, that certainly makes our little interlude in the elevator all the more...interesting."

To her immense satisfaction, Grant turned crimson again.

"I knew damned well you weren't a child then. Hell, no child would have—"

"What interlude in the elevator?"

Crista looked at Horace Blackburn, whose rabbity face wore a puzzled expression.

"I'll tell you what interlude," she snapped—and then she stopped. There was no way she could explain what had happened, not without Grant twisting the facts to make her seem the guilty party. "Never mind," she said stiffly. "We just—Mr. Landon and I had a difference of opinion, that's all."

"We still have a difference of opinion," Grant said coldly. "Miss Adams does not approve of me—and I most certainly do not approve of her."

"Miss Adams, Mr. Landon—please." Horace Blackburn rose from his chair. He was still smiling, but his face was shiny with sweat. "Please," he repeated, "if we could just get down to business...?"

Grant's expression was grim. "That's an excellent suggestion, Blackburn, especially since it's what I've been trying to do for days."

"Good, good. In that case, let's all sit down, shall we?"

Crista folded her arms over her breasts. Grant undid the button on his suit jacket and jammed his hands into his pockets. After a moment, Blackburn sighed and sank down into his chair.

"I'm sorry about the mix-up, Mr. Landon. Of course my secretary should have put you through to me in Italy. And she should have given you the Adams file."

"What Adams file?" Crista demanded.

Grant smiled tightly. "The one that would have told me you weren't twelve years old—among other things."

Crista gave him a withering look. "What business is it of yours how old I am?"

What business indeed? Grant thought. He didn't know if he wanted to put his fist through the wall or burst out laughing. Here he was, Crista Adams's guardian. All this time, he'd been thinking braces and boarding schools when it should have been bras and beauty salons—although, he thought with a sudden tightening of his body, he doubted if the woman he'd held in his arms in that elevator had need for either.

Incredible, he thought. He was responsible for a woman—not a child—a beautiful, reckless woman with the face of a Madonna, the temperament of a wildcat, the morals of a—a Jezebel. . . .

"Listen here," Crista said. Her voice was cold and hard and it drew the attention of both men. "Either I get answers, or I'm walking out that door." Her eyes flashed to Blackburn's face. "You've got five seconds, friend, starting now."

"My dear Miss Adams—"

"I am certainly not your 'dear' anything! And the countdown has already started. You've got three seconds left."

"Miss Adams—"

Crista snatched her purse from the chair. "So long, everybody. I'm out of here."

"All right!" Blackburn took a deep breath. "I can see that I am not going to be able to conduct this meeting as I'd planned. We are here to discuss the terms of your late uncle's will. I had thought to read it in its entirety, but it would seem—"

"Get to the bottom line, please." Grant shot back his cuff and looked at his watch. "I've a luncheon appointment, and I've no intention of missing it."

"And I have to get to work," Crista said tightly, "so if you—"

Grant laughed. Crista swiveled toward him, her eyes flashing.

"Does that amuse you, Mr. Landon? That some of us have to work for a living?"

"Not at all, Miss Adams. I was just wondering what sort of, ah, work it is that you do."

"Honest work," she snapped. "Something a man like you wouldn't understand."

Grant's gaze drifted slowly over her. Her hair hung wildly about her face, her raincoat was still damp in patches, and the broken boot heel made her stance uneven.

Even so, she looked untamed and magnificent, and he remembered how it had felt to hold her in his arms....

His jaw tightened. Damn, he thought, and he turned to Horace Blackburn.

"She's right, Blackburn. You've got five seconds. After that, you'll be sitting in this office and talking to yourself."

Blackburn took off his glasses, laid them on his desk, and rubbed the bridge of his nose.

"Very well. Miss Adams, as I'd indicated, we are here to deal with the last will and testament of your late uncle Simon." He paused. "As for Mr. Landon— he is here in lieu of his late father."

"Wonderful." Crista tapped her foot impatiently. "Why not go downstairs and invite some people off the street? I mean, if we're going to have a party—"

"You should be aware that Mr. Landon is a more than appropriate substitute, Miss Adams. He is a man of excellent standing in the community—"

"Hah!"

"And a member of the bar."

"So he's already told me. Would you like me to applaud?"

"Miss Adams—"

"Look, why don't I save us both a lot of time? I know why I'm here, Mr. Blackburn." She took a breath, wondering why what she was about to say suddenly seemed to put a lump in her throat. "You— you want to tell me that my uncle didn't leave me anything."

Blackburn's eyes rounded. "What? Oh, Miss Adams—"

"But that's fine. I didn't expect him to. I knew how he felt about me, and—and . . ."

Crista bit her lip. What was wrong with her? She hadn't wanted anything from Simon, not while he was alive, certainly not after his death. So why had her voice taken on this faint tremor?

She'd been a fool to have convinced herself that there'd be any pleasure in a face-to-face confrontation. Coming here had been a mistake, and it was time to put it behind her.

"Look," she said, "let's get this over with, okay? Read me what you have to read me, or let me sign whatever I have to sign, and—"

"Miss Adams." Blackburn's face took on a look of great solemnity. "Miss Adams, it is my duty to inform you that you are the sole heir to Simon Adams's estate."

The words seemed to echo through the room. She was what? Crista thought, staring at Horace Blackburn.

"I'm what?" she whispered.

"It's all yours," Blackburn said with another phony smile. "The house. The stock and bond portfolios. The real-estate holdings. You've just become a very wealthy young woman."

Crista groped behind her for the chair and then collapsed into it.

"But—but that's impossible," she murmured. "Uncle Simon didn't love me. He didn't even like me. He thought I was—that I was—"

"Indeed," Blackburn said. He was still smiling, but his voice was tinged with disapproval. "Nonetheless, you are the last direct descendant of the Adams bloodline. Your uncle could not bring himself to give away to strangers what generations of Adamses had amassed."

"Generous to the end," Crista said with a choked little laugh. She took a deep breath and looked at Blackburn. "I still don't believe it. There must be some mistake."

"There's no mistake, Miss Adams." Blackburn licked his lips. "But there is a proviso."

Grant's sharp bark of laughter cut across the attorney's words. Crista looked at him.

"Sorry," he said, but she could tell he was not sorry at all. "Go on, Blackburn," he said. "Tell her the rest."

Blackburn cleared his throat. "It's not at all an unusual proviso, Miss Adams. Many wills—especially when the inheritance is as large as this one—contain similar restrictions, and—"

Something cold seemed to twist inside Crista's belly. Whatever was coming, she was not going to like it.

"What restrictions?"

Blackburn picked up his glasses and carefully put them back on. Then he looked at Crista.

"Grant Landon is to be your guardian."

Somewhere inside the walls of Horace Blackburn's private office, a woman's voice rose in a quick burst of shrill laughter. It took Crista a moment to realize the laughter had come from her own throat.

A joke, she thought, staring blankly at her uncle's attorney, that's what this is. A very bad joke.

"You have—you have a strange sense of humor, Mr. Blackburn. All this, just to see if you can get a rise out of me?"

"Miss Adams, I assure you—"

"Well, let me tell you something." Crista's chair flew backward as she shot to her feet. "I don't think it's funny!"

"Believe me," Blackburn said stiffly, "I see no humor in this situation, either."

"Then—then what...?"

"What I've told you is true, Miss Adams. Your uncle willed everything to you."

"And—and the rest? The stuff about—about that man being my guardian...?" Crista swallowed dryly.

"That can't be right. Why would—I mean, how could—"

"Hell!" She turned as Grant came toward her, his eyes flat and cold, his mouth hard. He stopped in front of her, his powerful body blocking out everything else. "Let me lay it on the line for you, lady. Your uncle figured you'd get your hands on his money and blow it all. Isn't that right, Blackburn?"

"Yes. He was concerned that his niece—that you, Miss Adams, lack the maturity to—"

"So he decided to put a safety valve on his assets." A chilly smile twisted across Grant's lips. "And that's where I come in."

"You?" Crista took a breath. "But that's impossible! I don't even know you. And I'm not a child. You said yourself you thought I was twelve years old, but—"

"Never mind what I thought." Grant's eyes glittered. "You just became my ward. And you'll remain my ward until you reach your twenty-first birthday."

Crista stared at Grant's stony face. My God, she thought, he wasn't kidding!

Anger swept through her, swiftly shunting aside the shocked disbelief of the past few minutes.

"Like hell I will," she said through her teeth. Her eyes flashed as she spun toward Horace Blackburn. "There's no way that's going to happen, Horace! I am not a minor, and I am not a fool, and I will not be treated as if I were either! There's no law that says—"

"We're talking about the provisions of a will, Miss Adams. Your uncle had the right to make whatever provisions he deemed suitable concerning your inheritance. It was his money."

"But it's my life. Or have you 'gentlemen' conveniently forgotten that?"

Blackburn gave her a condescending smile. "Mr. Landon will be there to offer guidance—"

"Guidance? From him? I'd sooner take 'guidance' from a—from a snake!"

"Miss Adams, please. This is for your own good. Your uncle hoped that with maturity would come wisdom, and—"

"Wisdom?" She gave a hollow laugh. "I'm supposed to get wisdom in three months? Because that's when I'll be twenty-one, Horace. In just three short months."

"And three months is a very short time," Blackburn said soothingly. "You and Mr. Landon—"

"How did you pull this off?" Hands knotted into fists, Crista swung toward Grant and glared at him. "Just tell me that, okay? How did you get yourself appointed my guardian?"

Grant glowered at her from under his brows. "Don't be a complete fool," he growled. "I didn't even know who you were until an hour ago. If you think this has any more appeal for me than it has for you—"

"I'll get my own attorney, dammit!" Her chin lifted in angry defiance. "I'll take you to court, Landon, and I'll have this—this proviso tossed out the window!"

"That's your privilege," Grant said coldly. "Of course, by the time you get this case before a judge, you'll be blowing out the candles on your birthday cake—but that's up to you."

She stared at him, her face flushed, and then she turned back to Horace Blackburn.

"Let me get this straight. I inherited my uncle's estate—but until I'm twenty-one, that man is my guardian."

Blackburn nodded. "Exactly."

Her eyes narrowed. "And does it work in reverse? If I refuse the inheritance, I don't have to have anything to do with him?"

"I'm afraid I don't follow you, Miss Adams."

"It's really very simple." Crista snatched her purse from the chair and marched to the door. "Simon left me his money, and now I have to decide if it's worth putting up with that man to get it."

There was an instant's silence, and then Grant laughed. Crista swung toward him, her eyes shooting fire.

"Do you find this amusing?"

"You're good. Really good. I have to give you that."

"Don't give me anything, Mr. Landon. Just get out of my way!"

"Miss Adams—"

"And you stop 'Miss Adamsing' me, dammit!" Crista shrugged off Blackburn's restraining hand. "There's no law that says I have to accept the money, is there?"

Blackburn's brow furrowed. "Not exactly, but—"

"So, I was the last person in the world Simon could leave his money to, hmm? Well, that's too bad—because maybe I'm the last person in the world who wants it!"

"Like it or not, young woman, you are—by law— Simon Adams's heir. You cannot change that."

"But if I don't touch the money—"

"Whether you do or you do not, the facts will not change. Grant Landon is your legal guardian. You cannot just—"

"I can do anything I like! My uncle never figured that out, but I did, a long time ago."

"Yes." Grant's voice was low and chill. "I'll just bet you did."

Crista looked at him. "And just what is that supposed to mean?"

"It means you might as well be a child for all the maturity you show."

"I beg your pardon?" she said coldly.

"You heard me. From the minute you walked into this office, you've behaved like a spoiled brat."

"Which is it, Mr. Landon? Are you an attorney, or are you a shrink?"

"Just listen to yourself." Grant's mouth thinned as his eyes swept over her. "For that matter, just look at yourself. Everything you say and do is based on petulance."

"While you," Crista said with a brilliant smile, "act only out of cool, calm logic."

The gibe hit home. She knew he understood it as stripes of color bloomed on his cheekbones.

"I'm not proud of the times I haven't, I assure you," he said in a low, taut voice.

The memory of his kiss, of how she had responded to it, was bad enough. But to see the way he was looking at her now, to see the disgust in those hazel eyes as he remembered, too, was almost more than Crista could bear.

"Poor Grant," she said, fighting to keep her tone cool. "Led astray by the forces of evil. How sad."

"I'm glad you find this amusing, Crista. But I promise you—"

"I don't. I don't find it amusing at all!" Crista took a deep breath. "I find it—I find it incredible, that—that you, of all people, should set yourself up as a paragon of righteousness." She reached for the doorknob; her hand closed tightly around it. "You? My guardian?" She tossed her head, and the dark locks went flying. "It's like setting the fox to guard the henhouse!"

Crista flung open the door, stepped into the hall, and slammed it after her.

All things considered, it was a dignified exit—but once she was safely out of sight, she gave up the pretense of dignity.

She fled.

CHAPTER FOUR

As SOON as the door closed, Grant rounded on Horace Blackburn with barely repressed fury.

"Now, Mr. Landon," the other man said, but Grant cut him off in midsentence.

"Are you crazy, Blackburn? Making Crista Adams my ward—hell, the woman is no more a child than I am!"

"According to the law—"

"Dammit, don't go quoting the law to me!"

"I was merely going to point out that providing a guardian for an individual who has not yet attained the age of twenty-one—or even twenty-five—is perfectly within the bounds of legal precedent."

Grant eyed the other man coldly. "Don't play games, Counselor. I was led to believe I was going to assume responsibility for a child."

"Crista Adams needs a guiding hand, Mr. Landon. Look at the performance she just put on. What adult would pretend disinterest in such a fortune? Not that I believed her." Blackburn sank into his chair and folded his hands on his desk. "Give her time to think things over, and she'll be more than eager to get her hands on that money."

"That's not the point, dammit!" Grant gripped the beveled edges of Blackburn's desk and leaned over it. "It is absolutely ridiculous to make me her guardian. Crista can vote. She can drive. She can marry. She can get a passport and go anywhere she pleases. She can do any damned thing she wants to do—"

"Except spend her inheritance," Blackburn said smugly, "thanks to my foresight."

"Well," Grant said firmly, "you'll have to find someone else to play watchdog. I'm signing off."

"But I've already petitioned the court to accept you in lieu of your father. Surely—"

"Well, petition them again. As far as I'm concerned, if the lady wants to take her uncle's money and spend it on—on building retirement homes for shell-shocked schoolteachers, that's—"

"Simon Adams took his niece into his home when she was barely thirteen, Mr. Landon." Blackburn pursed his lips in a moue of distaste. "By then, I'm afraid, her character was formed."

"Listen, Blackburn, this is all very interesting, but. it has nothing to do with me, so—"

"Crista's mother was a dancer. Very beautiful and—how shall I put this?—very earthy. She raised the girl in her own image." Blackburn leaned forward. "Crista was out of control by the time she came into my client's home, Mr. Landon. She had a frivolous attitude, and as she grew older, she developed a love of...excess that greatly concerned him."

"Excess?" Grant said carefully.

"Yes. As soon as she...matured, she showed a disturbing habit of forming..." Blackburn paused delicately. "I suppose one might call them unfortunate relationships."

"I see." A muscle knotted in Grant's jaw. "With men, you mean."

Blackburn shrugged. "Looking the way she does, living in Greenwich Village—I shudder to think what kind of life she's leading."

Grant frowned. "She'll be twenty-one in—what did she say? Three months? Hell, it would take a miracle worker to make her develop a more responsible attitude by then."

Blackburn sighed with resignation. "I suppose you're right."

"Of course I'm right! And I want nothing to do with any attempts at turning a sow's ear into a silk purse!"

"Very well. I'll file a motion to request that someone else be put in your place."

"Good," Grant said. He could feel the weight lifting from his shoulders. "I'm certain there must be someone else. A family friend, or—"

"Oh, I'll take on the job myself." Blackburn rose to his feet and walked toward Grant, an oily smile curling across his mouth. "Actually," he said, "once I got a look at the girl today, I found myself rather envying you."

Grant's eyes narrowed. "There was nothing to envy, Blackburn. As her guardian, I'd have had only the most superficial dealings with Miss Adams. You know that."

"Of course." Blackburn closed one eye in a wink, and Grant thought once again how much the man resembled a rabbit. "But there's more than one way to—"

"No," Grant said with sudden coldness. "There's only one way—unless a man is ready to face the ethics committee and a disbarment hearing."

And, on that note, without so much as offering Horace Blackburn his hand, Grant stalked from the office.

By early evening, a cool breeze had blown away the rain clouds, although there was an almost unpleasant tension in the air, the sort that often precedes a storm. Grant was on the terrace of his penthouse, recuperating from the daily wars of his profession as the setting sun cast long shadows over Central Park.

He had traded his suit, wing-tip oxfords, pima cotton white shirt and maroon silk tie for softly faded jeans, a pair of beat-up running shoes, and a long-sleeved, ivory cotton sweater. He was sitting in his favorite bentwood chair, his feet propped on a hassock, and he had just taken what should have been the first satisfying swallow from a bottle of chilled India Pale ale.

But it wasn't satisfying. Nothing had been, the entire day. He'd felt overwound and irritable ever since that miserable meeting with Horace Blackburn.

And Crista Adams.

Grant put the bottle of ale on the table beside him and got to his feet. He sighed, walked to the railing, and gazed out over the park.

He had made his decision this morning.

"I'm not going to be Crista Adams's guardian," he'd told Horace Blackburn, and that was that.

So why was he still thinking about it?

Because he felt guilty as hell, that was why. It was bad enough that he'd come on to the woman in the first place, all but making love to her in an elevator. An elevator, for God's sake, he thought with a groan. He'd made a complete ass of himself. He knew it and

Crista Adams knew it—and now he was going to make things even worse by walking away from his responsibility and tossing her to the wolves.

Or to the rabbits. It all depended on how you viewed Horace Blackburn.

"Hell!"

Grant reached for the bottle of ale and tilted it to his lips, relishing the sting of the chilled liquid as it slid down his throat.

What did it matter? He didn't like Crista; he didn't owe her anything. And he had the definite feeling she was more than capable of handling Blackburn.

Grant shut his eyes. Blackburn's oily smile bloomed against the darkness of his lids and his beady little eye closed in a man-to-man wink.

"Damn!" Grant slammed down the ale bottle, and made his way through the apartment.

His driver was in the kitchen having after-dinner coffee and a slice of apple pie with the housekeeper, who looked up as Grant entered the room.

"Did you want your dinner now, sir?"

"No, thank you, Mrs. Edison, I'm not hungry. But I will need you for a while, Patterson." Grant took the Manhattan directory from next to the telephone and thumbed it open. Adams, he thought, Adams... Yes. There it was. "We're heading downtown, Patterson, to Greenwich Village."

Patterson's bushy eyebrows rose a fraction of an inch. "To the Village, sir?"

"Yes. To—" He frowned at the page. "To Thaler Street. Do you know it?"

"I do, sir."

Patterson's face revealed nothing, but Grant heard the careful shading in the man's voice.

"I take it that Thaler Street is not on the mayor's list of recommended tourist walks," he said dryly.

Patterson suppressed a grin. "You might say that, sir."

Grant sighed. "Take your time finishing your coffee, Patterson. It'll take me a few minutes to change."

In his bedroom, exchanging his jeans and sweater for a fresh white shirt and dark suit, Grant planned what he would say to Crista Adams.

Look, he'd tell her, it's obvious you're too old to be saddled with a guardian, and I certainly have no interest in telling you how to run your life. So let's behave like adults. For the next three months, if you make reasonable requests regarding your legacy, I'll approve them without hesitation. We won't even have to set eyes on each other. Everything can by done by telephone.

Yes, he thought, as he knotted his tie, that would do it. She would stay out of his way and he would stay out of hers. On her twenty-first birthday, they could shake hands, walk away from each other, and never look back.

Thank God he'd calmed down enough to view the situation logically.

"*How* much money did you say you inherited?"

Crista sighed. Until a few minutes ago, Danny hadn't known a thing about her past. But she'd blurted out the whole story when he'd stepped out of his bathroom, wearing nothing but a pair of snug-fitting jeans and a look of surprise at finding her home at six in the evening.

"Crista?" he'd said. "What's the matter?"

And she'd told him about her rich uncle and her inheritance, and now she was almost sorry she had because Danny was looking at her as if she were a weed that had suddenly turned into a rare orchid.

Still, who could blame him? It was all so fantastic and impossible. She'd tried her best not to think about it, to concentrate on work instead, but finally she'd tossed aside her order pad and told Gus she didn't feel well—which wasn't really much of an exaggeration, considering that her head had been pounding all day—and now here she was, trying to sound casual about having inherited a fortune...and having inherited Grant Landon's guardianship along with it, although she'd yet to tell Danny about that.

It was enough to make you laugh—or to make you cry, depending on your point of view. How could Fate do this, hand you enough money so you'd never have to worry about where the rent was coming from again and at the same time demand you give up your independence? Hand yourself over, mind and soul, to the one human being you most despised in the world—

"Crista?"

She blinked. Danny was sitting on the edge of the sagging sofa across from her, his eyes fixed on her face.

"How much did you say your uncle left you?"

"Millions," she said with a sigh. "Millions!"

"Yeah." Danny laughed and shook his head. "That's what I thought you said. So why do you look so upset?"

"Well," she said as she eased off her boots, "for one thing, I never expected it. Uncle Simon made it clear he'd never even look at me again if I left him." She rose and padded barefoot to the bedroom with

Danny trailing after her. "And then—well, there's this weird condition..."

Danny stopped in the doorway, turned his back to the room, and leaned against the jamb.

"What weird condition?"

Crista hesitated. It sounded so ridiculous even to think it... With a sigh, she peeled off her T-shirt and her leather skirt, then slipped a crimson-and-gold caftan over her head.

"Uncle Simon named a guardian to look after me."

Danny spun around. "You're joking!"

"I wish I were—but it's the truth." She flashed a weak smile over her shoulder as Danny followed her to the kitchen. "I've got a watchdog to make sure I stay on the straight and narrow until I turn twenty-one."

Danny straddled a chair and folded his arms along the back.

"Just like this old flick with James Mason," he said seriously. "Or was it Charles Laughton? There's this blonde babe, see, and—"

"I hate to disillusion you," Crista said with a little smile, "but this isn't a late-night movie." She reached under the sink, took out the kettle, and held it under the tap. "It's real life. *My* life!" Shaking her head, she set the kettle on the stove and turned on the burner. "Can you just picture it? I'm supposed to clear everything I do for the next three months with some iron-jawed guardian who's got a checkbook where his heart's supposed to be—"

"Hey, ease up. 'Guardian' is one of those code words, you know? Like 'stepmother'. People hear it, they think the worst. At least wait until you meet the guy. He's probably some harmless old dude who—"

"I *have* met him." Crista leaned back against the sink and dug her hands into the pockets of her caftan. "And I hated him on sight!"

Danny grinned. "Charles Laughton, not James Mason, huh?"

Crista thought of Grant's tall, imposing figure, his harshly handsome face, and she had to laugh.

"Well, in spirit," she said, "if not in body."

"Yeah, but so what? For three months you say 'may I?' and 'please', 'yessir' and 'nosir', and then, on your birthday, you say 'goodbye' and that's that."

"I suppose. It's just that this man—he—he..."

She frowned and gnawed lightly on her bottom lip. What could she say about Grant that wouldn't make her feel stupid? That he'd made love to her minutes after they'd met? That she didn't even like him, yet she'd trembled in his arms when she should have punched him in the jaw, that she'd come closer to surrender in that damned elevator than she'd ever come in her entire life...

"Crista?" Danny's eyes were riveted to hers. "Is there something you're not telling me?"

She hesitated. Danny was her friend. Her best friend. Maybe—maybe if she talked to him...

The downstairs bell shrilled, and Danny shot a glance at his watch.

"That's for me." He got to his feet. "I was supposed to meet some people... Look, babe," he said over his shoulder, "just give it a chance. Everything will work out."

Crista sighed as she followed after him. "I suppose."

"Just think how nice it's gonna be when you're rich," he said as he pressed the buzzer and then undid the lock and chain.

Her answering smile was tentative. "Well, I suppose. But—"

Danny put his hands lightly around her waist and turned her toward him.

"You could open a soup kitchen! The Village Community Center's been trying to do something like that for months. Or open a shelter and pick up every abandoned dog and cat you find."

Her smile grew. "I could, couldn't I?"

Danny went on with a smile, "And then you could tell Gus what he could do with his stupid restaurant— heck, you could *buy* the restaurant! Even turn it into a jewelry shop."

"Oh, Danny, you're right! I was so busy feeling sorry for myself...." Crista threw her arms around his neck just as the doorbell rang. "Thank you!"

Danny grinned mischievously. "You might even want to send a struggling young actor to England for the summer."

"You," Crista said, smiling up at him.

"Me," he said modestly as he reached behind her and threw open the door. "Hey, babe, now that you're gonna be filthy rich—"

"I wouldn't count on it."

The angry male voice drove the breath from Crista's lungs. She went still in Danny's arms, then spun around.

Grant was standing in the open doorway. For just an instant, her heart kicked against her ribs at the sight of him, tall and dark and so overwhelmingly masculine—but then she saw the look of distaste on his lips and her spine straightened.

"What are you doing here?" she said coldly.

"Such a warm welcome, Crista." His eyes narrowed as he took in the scene. "I can see I've come at an inopportune time."

Hell, he thought, that was one way of putting it. The little tableau before him was about as intimate as possible—Crista in that silky robe in colors that should have been garish but instead only made her look more beautiful, the man holding her with all that bare skin and muscle showing above a pair of unfastened jeans.

A cold knot tightened in his belly. Were Crista and her lover coming from bed? Or were they on their way to it?

Grant's lips drew back from his teeth. "Perhaps you'd like to introduce me to your—friend."

A flush rose in Crista's face. "I asked you a question, Grant. What are you doing here?"

"Crista?" Danny's voice was low. "You want me to tell this guy to beat it?"

Crista lifted her hand and put it over Danny's.

"Danny," she said quickly, "this is Grant Landon." She swallowed dryly. "My—my guardian."

She could feel Danny's jolt of alarm. "*This* guy is your guardian?"

"Yes." She tilted her chin up. "And he was just about to tell me why he's come here—weren't you, Mr. Landon?"

Grant took a deep breath. It took effort, but he finally managed what he hoped was a smile.

"I came to discuss some important business with you."

"Business? You and me?" Crista laughed with derision. "I don't think so."

Grant's mouth thinned. "It would be to your advantage to listen to what I have to say, Crista."

"Have you decided to sign off as my guardian?"

"If I did, someone else would take my place."

Crista shrugged off Danny's hands and took a step forward. "Even that would be an improvement."

"Dammit, Crista! Stop being such a little fool and—"

"That's enough, pal!" Danny's words were a growl of warning.

Grant's eyes shot to the man's face. "If you're smart, *pal*," he said, his voice very soft and very cold, "you'll keep out of this."

"If you think you can come down here and push Crista around..."

"This matter doesn't concern you. It's between my ward and me."

"I am not your ward," Crista said fiercely.

"But you are. The sooner you get that through your head, the better."

"And don't use that tone with me!"

Grant's brows rose. "What tone?"

"The one that makes it sound as if I need humoring!" Crista's hands balled into fists. "There's nothing in my uncle's will that gives you the right to—to come barging into my home! You are not welcome here. Furthermore, I'm—I'm busy!"

"Yes." Grant's gaze swung from Crista to Danny. "I can see that."

"Good." Crista put her hands on her hips. "Then you won't mind leaving."

"After we've talked. In private."

"Crista," Danny muttered, "I swear, if you want me to take care of this guy—"

"Take care of me?" Grant said very softly. His lips drew back from his teeth in a quick, feral smile. "What a quaint phrase. What, exactly, did you have in mind?"

"Stop it!" Crista blew out her breath. "This is ridiculous. Grant, if you've anything to say, say it now."

Grant's muscles tensed with rage. Jesus, what was happening to him? The boy was Crista's lover; it didn't take a genius to figure that out. And he had every right to want to protect her—hell, in another life, Grant would have commended him for it...

But not in this life. Not while Crista was standing so close to him that he could smell the faint scent of violets that clung to her skin, not while he could see the little pulsebeat in her throat...

He gave Danny a smile that was easy, almost lazy. "Did you know that she's not yet twenty-one?"

"Dammit, Grant! I am of age to—to—"

Crista bit her lip. I am of age to choose my own friends, she'd almost said—but suddenly she realized how this must look to Grant, she in her robe and Danny in those jeans—and it was perfect. Perfect! She might be Grant Landon's ward—but she was not a child he could intimidate.

And what better way to remind him than to make sure he went on thinking exactly as he was?

With a look of defiance, she half turned to Danny and put her hand lightly on his bare chest.

"I am of age to choose my own lovers!"

She felt Danny's body twitch with surprise, but—bless him—he kept silent.

"Of course," Grant said. "You are, indeed, old enough to make certain choices." His smile sent a flicker of warning up her spine. "Just as it is my duty to make others."

"Dammit, don't talk in riddles! Say what you came to say and then go!"

Grant looked at Danny. "Do you live here, Mr....?"

"Amato." Danny smiled contemptuously. "Of course I live here."

"You don't have to answer any of his questions," Crista said sharply. "Where you live isn't his concern."

"Ah, but as your guardian, the expenditure of your funds is very much my concern." Grant smiled politely. "If you were the sole occupant of this apartment, Crista, we'd have to find a tenant to take over your lease. You do have a lease, don't you?"

"What are you talking about?"

The simple question almost stopped Grant in his tracks. What in hell *was* he talking about? He had come to tell Crista that he was not going to interfere in her life, to assure her that he would be nothing more obtrusive than a voice on the phone for the next three months.

But that had all changed. Seeing her this way, standing in the embrace of her half-naked lover, her eyes blazing with defiance, had erased any rational thought from his mind.

Dammit, the woman really did need someone to watch out for her! Everything that had happened today, from the way she'd behaved hours ago to finding her now, living in squalor with a man who was not just sleeping with her but was already asking her for money—all of it screamed the same undeniable message.

Crista Adams needed a firm, guiding hand—and that hand would have to be his.

His brothers had accepted their burdens without complaint. Well, it was time he did the same. No matter how he disliked it, he had a responsibility. And he would not—could not—shirk it.

Grant took a deep breath. "I came here to see, firsthand, what sort of living arrangements you had."

"Well, you've seen. And now, if you don't mind, Danny and I—"

"I find those arrangements unacceptable."

She stared at him for a moment while her brain processed the sentence, and then her dark brows lifted.

"Am I supposed to burst into tears at that?"

Grant smiled tightly. "Get dressed, Crista."

"I've no intentions of getting dressed. Danny and I planned a quiet evening at home, and—"

"Get dressed," he repeated, "and pack your things."

"What are you talking about?"

"For the next three months, you are my responsibility."

"You mean, for the next three months, I'm stuck with you!"

"As you prefer." Grant's eyes met hers. "The point is, you are not going to spend those months here."

"Don't be crazy. You can't just tell me where to—"

"I can," he said, "and I am. Now, get moving."

It was pure bluff, and he knew it—but would she? Grant stood expressionless, his eyes on Crista's face. Finally, she gave a little sob of rage.

"You—you miserable rat! You—you..."

Her voice broke. Suddenly, she looked terribly lost and alone. Grant wanted to go to her, take her in his arms, and stroke the glossy black waves of hair back from her flushed face. It's all right, he wanted to say, it's all right, Crista. I won't let anything hurt you.

"Crista?" Danny slid his arms around her. "This guy can't really do this, can he?"

Grant's spine stiffened. "Where did you get your law degree, pal?" he snapped, and then he completely abandoned whatever ethics he had left. "As her guardian, I can do whatever I damned well please. Now, go on, Crista. I'll give you five minutes—and then I'll carry you out of here in that robe!"

He saw the rage flicker in her eyes. She drew in her breath as if she were going to say something, but then she clamped her lips together, turned, and stalked down the corridor. A door slammed, and then there was silence.

Moments passed. Then, at last, the sound of swift, feminine footsteps came tapping down the hallway.

Grant's teeth ground together. Crista was dressed exactly as she had been that morning, in that damnable little skirt and tight T-shirt. The boots had been fixed, he saw, and rose, just as he'd remembered them, almost to her thighs. She had a small suitcase in one hand—and a cardboard carrier in the other.

He frowned. "What," he said with a nod toward the carrier, "is that?"

The answer came in the form of a long, mewing cry.

"A cat?" Grant said. Crista didn't answer. "That's out of the question. You cannot take a cat with you."

Her eyes met his, blazing with defiance. "Try and stop me!"

She turned to Danny and kissed his cheek. Then, head high, she marched out the door. After a moment, Grant followed. Even an attorney with no ethics knew when it was time to retreat.

The cat, and that abominable outfit, could be dealt with later. All that mattered now was that he had taken Crista out of that rattrap... and out of her lover's arms.

For the next three months, she would live with him, Grant thought, and even as he did, he despised himself for the sudden, quicksilver race of fire he felt shoot through his blood.

CHAPTER FIVE

CRISTA was not a stranger to luxury and money. It was what she'd been surrounded and suffocated by all the years she'd lived with her uncle.

Even so, Grant's penthouse took her by surprise.

It was enormous, easily twice the size of Uncle Simon's town house, and stunningly elegant. The sea of white that stretched before her might have come straight from the pages of a magazine.

But it was hard to imagine someone actually living here and putting their feet up while they read the Sunday papers.

Grant's housekeeper greeted them without a blink, as if outlandishly dressed women clutching cardboard carriers that gave off terrifying hisses and moans were everyday events in her life.

"Mrs. Edison," Grant said, "this is Miss Adams." He took Crista by the arm and drew her forward. "Please show her to the guest suite and see to it she's comfortable."

"Certainly, sir."

"You can put that in the laundry room," he said, jerking his head toward the carrier. "And then—"

"My cat comes with me!"

The words burst from Crista's lips. Grant gave her a patient smile.

"And so he has—against my better judgment. Now it's time to let Mrs. Edison have him."

Crista's chin rose in defiance. "Sweetness stays with me."

Sweetness? Grant's gaze flew to the carrier box. The creature making those bloodcurdling sounds was named Sweetness? Hell, he thought wearily, why not? Everything else about this endless day was crazy; if his ward turned out to be a sexy hellion with an inheritance worth millions instead of a poor little waif, why couldn't a cat that screamed like a banshee be named Sweetness?

God in heaven, who would believe any of this? Cade and Zach were out in the real world, dealing with real problems, and he—he was debating feline rights with a woman whose attitude made the cat's hissing sound like murmurs of love.

Enough was enough. This was his home, and he was her guardian, and that was the end of it.

"I am not going to argue with you, Crista," he said with a brisk certitude as he reached for the carrier. "Now, hand that thing over!"

"No!"

Grant's eyes narrowed. "Mrs. Edison will fix it a sleeping place for the night, and then, in the morning, I'll arrange for it to be sent to—"

"It's not an 'it', it's a 'he'. And you're not sending him anywhere."

"Stop being a little fool!" Grant could feel his temper rising. "This is no place for a cat."

"This is no place for a human being, either," Crista snapped, tossing her head so that her hair flew back from her flushed cheeks. "Or hadn't you noticed?"

"Stop this nonsense!" Grant snatched the pet carrier from her hand. "The animal will be perfectly comfortable in a kennel."

"He won't. Try putting yourself in his place. How would you feel if you were suddenly uprooted, taken from your home and—and set down in a—a strange place without anyone to—to care for you or—or..."

To her absolute dismay, Crista felt the swift, humiliating sting of tears start in her eyes. She blinked furiously, praying Grant hadn't noticed that momentary sign of weakness, and took a steadying breath.

"You're right," she said coolly. "Now that I think about it, he would be better off in a kennel. That way I won't have to worry about his shedding or leaving footprints in this—this interior decorator's showplace!" Her chin rose. "Now, if you don't mind, I'd like to go to my room."

There was a moment's silence, and then Grant nodded. "Mrs. Edison, see Miss Adams to her rooms, will you?"

"Yes, sir." The housekeeper cleared her throat and nodded toward the cat carrier Grant was clutching in his hand. "Ah, shall I take care of that first, or—"

"No." Grant cleared his throat, too. "No, it can wait," he said. "I'll just take the thing to the laundry room and you can deal with it later." He looked at Crista. "Good night."

She didn't answer. Instead, she turned and followed Mrs. Edison across the foyer to the curving white staircase, her head high, her shoulders square. Grant watched her until she'd vanished; then, still holding the cardboard carrier, he made his way to the laundry room, switched on the light, shut the door, and put the box on the tiled floor.

The humming and hissing noises had stopped, but he had no idea why. It might be a good idea to check before Mrs. Edison opened the box. He bent, undid the closure, and waited. After a second or two, a gray head pushed its way cautiously into the light.

It was a cat, all right, with a healed but mangled ear, and all the noise had clearly been nothing but a bluff, for he could see that it was trembling.

Grant shook his head, bent again, and lifted the cat gingerly in his hands.

All that fuss for this?

The cat looked at him, its huge yellow eyes unblinking, and then it gave a delicate little shudder.

Grant's jaw tightened. "Hell," he said again, and then he wrenched open the door.

Mrs. Edison was coming down the steps as he started up.

"There you are, sir. I've settled the young lady in as best I could and..." Her voice trailed away as she saw the cat. "Oh, the sweet little..."

Her eyes flew to Grant's, and he frowned.

"The damned thing will probably destroy the laundry room, left to its own devices," he growled.

"Yes, sir."

"Find a box somewhere and line it with an old towel. And I suppose you'd better fill a saucer with milk."

"With tuna fish, sir. Milk's not really..." Mrs. Edison looked at Grant, swallowed, and nodded her head. "Of course, Mr. Grant. I'll take care of everything."

Still glowering, he strode down the hall and pounded his fist against the door to the guest suite. It swung open immediately.

"Mrs. Edison? I wonder if you could just remember to give my cat a dish of—"

Crista stared in disbelief. She had expected the housekeeper to be standing there, but it was Grant instead. His face was dark as a thundercloud—and he was holding Sweetness by the scruff of his neck.

"Here," he said, thrusting the cat at her. "Take the damned thing and be done with it!"

Crista snatched the cat into her arms. She buried her face in its fur. When she looked up, her eyes were shining.

"You mean—" she swallowed "—you mean, I can have him with me tonight?"

"I mean," Grant said coldly, "that you can keep him. Just make sure he stays in your rooms."

She nodded.

"I'm not doing this for you," Grant said brusquely. "I'm doing it because I can't afford any more disruptions in my life. I know you may find this difficult to believe, Crista, but I have a law practice to attend to. You are not my only legal responsibility, and—"

"Grant?"

Her voice was soft, yet it cut through him sharply enough to cause a curious pain in his chest. She was wearing those silver earrings again, the ones with the little bells; they were swaying ever so slightly, their soft, tinkling sound almost like a sigh.

"I—I want to thank you. For understanding about the cat, I mean." She swallowed; his gaze flew to the long, tender column of her throat, then returned to her face. There was a hint of dampness on her cheeks and a faint tremor in her lips.

Was she going to cry?

"He means a great deal to me. I—I found him, you see, in the street. He'd been hurt, and . . ."

Her voice droned on, as soft as the cat's fur had been under his hand. Grant jammed his hands into his pockets; it was ridiculous, but he wanted to reach out, take her in his arms, and tell her everything would be fine...

He felt his heart harden.

Oh, but she was good at this, at making a man see her as he wished she were. But why wouldn't she be? She'd had lots and lots of practice.

"...and you won't have to worry," she said. "I promise. I'll see to it he stays in my room and doesn't—"

"Make sure that you do. If I so much as glimpse him where he shouldn't be, all the pleading in the world won't help you. The cat will be out of here so fast it'll make your head spin."

He turned sharply and walked away. No, Crista thought, as she stared after him, no, he didn't walk. He marched.

Her lips tightened. She bumped the door with her hip, slamming it shut, then leaned back against it.

How stupid could she have been? For just a moment, she'd almost thought he might be human.

But he wasn't, and she would not make the same mistake again.

"Three months, Sweetness," she whispered. The cat purred and tapped a gentle paw against Crista's chin. "That's right, little one. So long as we have each other, we can certainly manage to get through twelve weeks."

And that was all it was. Twelve short weeks.

Then why did it seem like a lifetime?

* * *

By morning, she had figured out the way to make the time pass instead of drag.

She had a life, and she would go on living it. Oh, she'd give up her job, though it was tempting to keep Gus's leather outfit, wear it as often as she could manage just to see Grant's mouth narrow with distaste, but only a masochist would want to go on tending tables at the restaurant when she didn't have to.

As for the rest—her volunteer work at the community center and animal shelter, her sketching and her jewelry design—Crista's mouth firmed. She wasn't about to give up any of it. Not for a million Grant Landons!

She dressed quickly, pulling on a pair of ribbed black tights, a black turtlenecked sweater, and black ballet flats. She draped a necklace of her own making around her neck—a long length of brightly colored trade beads interspersed with silver squash blossoms—put on the silver-bell earrings, and brushed out her hair.

It was almost nine according to her watch. Grant would certainly be gone by now.

Crista plucked the hated leather skirt, boots, and T-shirt from the chair where she'd left them the night before and stuffed them into a canvas carryall bag. Then she patted Sweetness, stepped out into the corridor, and closed the door carefully after her.

The apartment was silent, the dense white carpet muffling her footsteps as she made her way down the steps.

Mrs. Edison was cleaning the living room, although what dust would dare settle in such sterile surroundings was beyond Crista to imagine.

"Oh, my," she said with a little laugh, "you startled me, Miss Adams. Did you want something? You had only to ring, and I—"

"I'm going out for a while, Mrs. Edison. If *you* want something, I'd be glad to pick it up for you."

The housekeeper stared at her. "Me?"

"Something from the market, perhaps. Milk, or bread . . . whatever."

"No. No, thank you very much. But, ah, Mr. Landon didn't—he didn't mention that you'd be— that you—"

Crista's smile faded. "I don't have to clear my comings and goings with anyone, Mrs. Edison."

"Well, no. I suppose not. But if he should phone and ask after you . . ."

"Just tell him I'm out."

"Yes, but—"

"Goodbye, Mrs. Edison."

It was sunny out, and warm, and Crista's sense of well-being grew with every step she took. Even the subway ride down to the Village was exhilarating.

Freedom, she thought with a little smile, was a wonderful thing!

Gus's Tavern was quiet at that hour. Crista made her way straight to his office and knocked on the door.

"Come," Gus barked.

He looked up from his racing form as she stepped inside and listened with disinterest as she began explaining that she was quitting.

"Yeah, yeah," he said, leaning back in his chair and scratching his chest. "So?"

"I just wanted to thank you, for taking me on in the first place, and—"

"Hey, don't bother with the bull, girl. You're quitting. That means I ain't gonna give you no references." He chuckled at his own joke, then frowned as she piled the skirt, boots, and pink shirt on his desk. "What's that for?"

"For the next girl who needs them." Crista smiled slightly. "Give the stuff to her and wish her luck for me."

Out on the street again, she found it was all she could do to keep from flinging out her arms and whirling in a circle. Danny had tried making her see how terrific it was, inheriting all this money, but she'd been so angry at Grant that she hadn't really been listening.

Now, for the first time, reality was sinking in. She was done with surly customers, greasy food, and the stink of stale beer. And if that meant putting up with Grant Landon for a couple of months, well, so what? She had put up with worse when she'd lived with Uncle Simon.

Try as he might, Grant would not manage to spoil her happiness!

She strolled the streets in contentment, glad to be back where she'd spent not just the past six months of her life but her childhood. Her parents had had little money—dancers and painters were rarely rich—but her life had been full and happy.

And it would be again, she thought with determination, once her time in purgatory had ended.

She stopped off at both the animal shelter and the community center to pledge more volunteer hours, and then, since it was such a lovely afternoon, she bought herself lunch from a vending cart and sat munching her hot dog and sipping her Coke on a bench near the Washington Arch, listening as a long-haired young man with a battered guitar sang mournfully of love won and lost.

Finally, as the afternoon wore to a close, she paid a visit to her apartment. Danny was out, but it was still good to be back in the familiar, shabby rooms. Crista stuffed her sketch pad and some unfinished jewelry into her canvas bag, hesitated over her tools and a small reel of silver wire, then tucked them in, too.

It was hard, imagining she could ever find a place to work in the pristine whiteness of Grant's penthouse, but perhaps just having her things with her would make her feel better.

It was late as she made her way toward the front door of Grant's apartment building, and her footsteps quickened. It had been a lovely day, and the last thing she wanted to do was spoil it with a confrontation...

"Miss Adams?"

She looked up. The doorman—a different one from those she'd seen before—was looking at her questioningly.

"Yes?"

He smiled politely. "I'm glad to see you, miss."

Crista's answering smile was puzzled. "That's very kind of you, but—"

"If you'd just come with me, please?"

As if she had a choice, Crista thought, her smile dimming as he escorted her to the penthouse elevator. She'd forgotten you needed your own key. Well, Grant would simply have to—

She had a quick glimpse of the doorman reaching for the intercom as the doors slid shut, and suddenly she knew what to expect when they opened again.

Grant. Grant, you bastard!

He was waiting for her, his face hard, his mouth tight and thin.

"Where in hell have you been?"

Crista thought of half a dozen answers and discarded them all in favor of a cool smile.

"Good evening to you, too," she said, and started past him.

She hadn't gotten two feet when Grant's hand closed on her shoulder.

"I asked you a question," he said, spinning her toward him.

"You didn't ask me a question. You started an inquisition." She jerked away from him, her head high. "And you can just play that tune to yourself, Torquemada."

He caught her again at the door to her room. "How dare you disappear? I did not give you permission to—"

"Dare? Permission?" She swung around and glared at him, feeling the lovely day falling away from her with the speed of sound. "*You* didn't give *me* permission?"

"You heard me! As long as I'm in charge—"

"You're not in charge of anything—except my money. If you think you can—"

She gasped as he shoved her inside the room. The door slammed shut after him.

"Where were you all day?"

"It's none of your business!"

"Were you in the Village?"

"What if I was? I don't have to—"

"Greenwich Village," he said with disdain. "Hell, I might have known."

His eyes raked over her, from head to toe and back again. She was dressed all in black, the bulkiness of her sweater only emphasizing the long, curved line of her legs; she was draped with silver and beads, those damned silver-bell earrings of hers tinkling softly and swaying against the ebony silk of her hair....

Grant's gut clenched. She looked wild and un-tamed, and suddenly he ached to haul her into his arms and—and...

He took a step back and jammed his hands into his pockets.

"What kind of outfit is that? Dammit to hell, don't you own a decent dress?"

Crista slung down her canvas bag and slapped her hands on her hips.

"Tell the truth," she said with a cold smile. "You were hoping for another chance to drool over my leather boots!"

"Me? Drool over those boots? You've got to be joking."

"Well, then, it won't bother you to know that they're gone."

"Gone? What do you mean, gone?"

She hesitated. Now was the time to tell him; to say, well, the boots, the whole ridiculous outfit, was never anything I'd ever really wear in the first place. It was all just something I wore, like a uniform...

"Well?" Grant's scowl deepened. "What do you mean, they're gone?"

"I know you're going to find this hard to believe, but I hated those boots. And that skirt. I only wore it because Gus—"

"Gus?" he said, his eyes narrowing.

"Yes, Gus. He—"

"Who the hell is Gus?"

"I'm trying to tell you, dammit! Gus has this—this thing about girls wearing boots, and short skirts, and..."

She saw the look that came over his face. Damn you, Grant Landon, she thought, damn you for leaping to conclusions, for judging me, and damn me for ever thinking of trying to tell you the truth.

"...and I figured, it doesn't matter what he likes now," Crista said, her eyes cool. "So I decided to give him the whole outfit for his next girl."

"For—his—next—girl," Grant repeated through his teeth.

"Yes. Why not? I don't need the stuff anymore. Someone else might as well have it."

His hands fell hard on her shoulders. "How many men are there in your life? Do you know, or don't you bother keeping count?"

"My life, and the men in it, are none of your concern."

"What you do is very much my concern, and don't you forget it." His face darkened. "The trouble is, *I'm* the one who keeps forgetting. Hell, you'd think I'd know by now that you and morality are complete strangers."

Crista wrenched away from him. "Just listen to you, preaching morality! After yesterday, in that elevator..." Her voice trembled with anger. "I didn't notice you worrying about anybody's morals then!"

He'd set himself up for that, and he knew it. But she was as guilty as he was. Hell, she was guiltier.

"Well? What's the matter, Grant? Did I finally get through to you?"

"Listen, lady, I never pretended I was a candidate for sainthood." He thrust his face toward her, his eyes cold as glass. "You were advertising what you have and I was in the mood to try it."

"You bastard! You were acting like a—like a gorilla! You were—you were all over me—"

"Yes." His hands slid to her waist. "I was. And you loved every minute of it."

"Liar!"

He pulled her hard against him, reveling in the feel of her soft breasts against his chest and her rounded hips against his pelvis. "I could have pulled up your skirt and taken you against that wall."

Crista slammed her fists against his chest. "Never!"

He laughed as his hands slid into her hair, easing beneath the black, silky strands, tilting her face to his.

"Never?"

"You're damned right, never!"

She cried out as he bent to her and claimed her mouth in a kiss that was hot with anger.

"Stop lying to yourself, Crista. You wanted the same thing I did."

"It's not true! I didn't. I don't—"

"Yes. You do." The anger was fading from his voice and something else was replacing it. She could see it in his eyes, feel it echoing to the beat of her heart.

She shuddered when she saw his eyes darken, and his arms began to tighten around her. "Crista," he whispered. "Crista—kiss me the way you did yesterday."

She couldn't hide it, the torrent of desire that was sweeping over her. He saw it, felt it as she swayed unsteadily in his arms, and he bent his head quickly, his breath whispering over her lips in the barest hint of a kiss.

Her hands lifted toward him, then fell away.

"No," she said, but his mouth was at her throat, seeking out the pulse point where her blood leaped with the reality of her need. "Grant," she said, "Grant, listen—"

"I am," he said. She moaned as he cupped her breast. "I'm listening to every word you say. And I know that you want this as much as I do."

She shook her head. "No. No, it's—it's insane."

It was. It was the worst kind of insanity—but oh, she ached for him. For the feel of his hands, the heat of his kiss, the strength of his enfolding arms.

With a cry of surrender, Crista threw her arms around Grant's neck and drew his head down to hers.

The kiss was fire, a flame that threatened to consume them both. Grant's thumb moved across her breast, urging the nipple to sweet, swollen fullness.

"Tell me what you want," he said thickly. "Tell me, Crista."

He watched her eyes turn to smoke as he waited for her answer. Her lips were parted, softly swollen from his kisses. Her skin was flushed with desire.

Dammit! Grant's breath caught. What was he waiting for? What did he want her to say? That she wanted him more than she'd wanted Danny? Or Gus?

Or any of the other faceless men who had possessed her?

With an anguished groan, he thrust Crista from him, wrenched open the door, and welcomed the return of his sanity.

CHAPTER SIX

GRANT sat on the terrace early the next morning. The sun was beating down on his shoulders and, thanks to the tropical disturbances far to the south in the Caribbean, the air felt oppressively thick.

He was drinking coffee, trying to convince himself it was not the black sludge it seemed to be.

He'd made it himself after he'd finally given up all pretence at sleep and gone for his daily run around the Central Park reservoir at an hour when sensible people, including Mrs. Edison, were still in their beds.

The run had helped. The coffee, miserable though it was, had helped, too, and now, after a sleepless night of wondering whom he despised more, himself or the woman in his guest room, things were finally coming into the proper perspective.

Grimacing, he put down the cup, got to his feet, and strolled the length of the terrace, his hands tucked into the pockets of his running shorts, his eyes focused on the skyline.

Last night, he'd bolted from Crista's room like a man escaping a bad dream, gone straight as an arrow for the bar in the library, and poured himself a shot of brandy that he'd tossed down as if it were water. The stuff had burned his throat, proving that even fifty-year-old booze could taste like rotgut if you drank it the wrong way.

But the brandy had done its job, clearing his head and bringing back at least a glimmer of common sense. By the time he'd climbed the stairs to his bedroom, he'd known that it was time to cut the pretense.

He'd have horsewhipped a man who took on the responsibility of being a woman's guardian and then behaving as he had.

It was time to walk away from this mess and not look back.

He made his way to his chair, sank into it, and picked up his coffee cup. Walk away, he thought. Yeah, that was the ticket. If he didn't—if he didn't...

He took a mouthful of coffee and shuddered.

Look what had almost happened last night.

What in hell had come over him? He had never in his life wanted a woman who didn't want him, never forced himself on one...

But he hadn't forced himself on Crista. No matter how she pretended, he could see the desire burning in her eyes like a fire storm when he touched her.

Okay. Maybe that was her thing. Maybe she got turned on by that kind of sexual insanity.

But he wasn't, dammit! He never lost himself, not in sex or anything else. Self-control was what he was all about. Even his father had recognized that.

"I know you hate my guts, boy." That had been Charles's favorite taunt for so many years. "Why don't you just admit it?"

But Grant had never given him what he wanted, never broken down or responded. He knew a shrink would probably say that that steadfast refusal to react to his father's provocation had been his own form of rebellion, but whatever the reason, it had served him well, first as a boy and then as a man.

And yet, he'd almost lost all that taut self-discipline last night—and for what? For a woman he didn't even like, a woman any man could have.

It was crazy—and he was going to put a stop to the craziness right now. He was only waiting for the hands of the clock to reach a reasonable hour and then he'd call Sam Abraham, one of his law partners, and set things in motion.

Sam would make the perfect guardian. He was old enough to be wise, invariably pleasant, and he had a couple of grandchildren Crista's age. If Sam agreed to assume her guardianship—and Grant was sure he would—the court would almost definitely agree, too.

It was just that he'd never walked away from anything in his life, and it galled him to admit defeat.

He sighed. Was it really only a little while since he and Cade and Zach had laughed over the easy job he'd been stuck with? It had all seemed so simple then, with their hands joined in that old Deadeye Defenders pledge.

Cade was having his own troubles down in Texas; he'd called days ago, sounding grim. And Zach had ended up stuck out in Hollywood longer than he'd expected, but he had to be having a ball. He had a suite in a cushy hotel where the starlets probably filled the swimming pool from one end to the other.

On impulse, Grant put down his coffee cup and reached for the phone. He dialed, then waited, and finally a voice mumbled something that might have been hello.

"Zach?"

"Yeah. Who the hell is this?"

Grant chuckled, sat back, and stretched out his legs. He felt better already.

"Is that any way to say hello to your big brother?"

Zach groaned into the phone. "Grant?"

"On the nose, buddy. How're you doing?"

There was another groan, followed by a deep sigh. "Grant, you jerk, do you have any idea what time it is?"

"Sure." Grant glanced at his watch. "It's two minutes after seven, and..." He blinked. "Damn!"

"Yeah," Zach said wearily. "You got that right."

"Oh, man, I'm sorry! I forgot about the time difference. What is it out there—4:00 a.m.?"

"Uh-huh." Zach's voice was stronger now; Grant could imagine him sitting up against the pillows, rubbing his eyes. "And I only got to bed a couple of hours ago."

Grant smiled. "Party time, huh?"

There was a moment's pause. "Not exactly."

"Hey, pal, if you're doing business until the wee small hours—"

"Grant? Why are you calling?"

Zach sounded abrupt, but who could blame him? It was four in the morning. *Four in the morning?* Grant shook his head. He was really in bad shape! How could he have made such a dumb mistake?

"I swear to God, Grant, if this is some gag you and Cade cooked up..."

"No. No, it's not a gag. It's..." Grant took a breath. "I suppose it sounds crazy, but I was sitting here, thinking about—about things, and—and—"

And, all of a sudden, he knew exactly why he'd phoned.

"Zach? You remember once we were talking about how to score in the market?"

"You called me at this hour for stock market advice?"

Grant laughed a little. "No, no. It's just—you said—you once said something that stayed with me, that only the true believers and the certifiably insane didn't know when it was time to cut their losses and get out."

"So?" Zach chuckled. "My clients pay a lot of money for that kind of advice."

"It's good advice, isn't it?" Grant switched the phone to his other ear and leaned forward. "I mean, you wouldn't—you wouldn't think a man was admitting defeat if—if he put it to use?"

There was a silence before Zach spoke. "Listen, Grant, what's going on? Have you run into financial trouble?"

"No. Hell, no. It's just—you remember this deal I walked into, this guardianship?"

"The twelve year old kid. Sure."

"The thing is, she's not twelve."

"Younger?"

"Older. Lots older. And..." Grant hesitated. "She's not a girl at all, Zach. She's a woman, and—"

"And," Zach said, his voice suddenly harsh, "she's doing a number on your head."

Grant gave a little laugh. "That's the simple way of putting it."

"*Cherchez la femme!*"

"What?"

"I said—"

"I know what you said. Look for the woman. But what's that got to do with—"

"Wherever there's trouble, there's a dame. You can count on it." Zach blew out his breath. "Listen, man, do yourself a favor. Hand the babe off to somebody else."

"Yeah. I thought of that. But dammit, I signed on for this and—"

"Well, sign off! Remember? Cut your losses." Zach gave a choked laugh. "It's such good advice I might just take it myself."

Grant frowned. "Are you talking about that production company?"

"Yeah," Zach said, his voice flat, "of course. What else would I be talking about? Listen, brother mine, I've got a breakfast meeting with a bunch of West Coast sharks. If I'm gonna be my usual brilliant self, I need at least a couple of hours of shut-eye."

Grant smiled. "Okay."

"Okay." Zach cleared his throat. "And Grant? I'm serious about cutting your losses. Do it—while you still can."

"Thanks for the advice. You stay well, you hear?"

"Yeah. You, too."

Grant hung up the phone and leaned back in his chair. When they were kids, his brothers had often turned to him for advice, but it was such a long time since he'd had to ask anyone for an opinion that he'd almost forgotten how to do it.

Talking with Zach had made him feel better. In fact, he'd phone Sam Abraham right now and—

The phone rang as he reached for it, and he grinned.

"Listen, Zach," he said, "you don't have to worry. I'm going to do what you said and—"

But it wasn't Zach calling, it was Horace Blackburn—and by the time Grant hung up the telephone, he knew that his brother's advice had come one day too late.

* * *

Crista had spent a sleepless night, too, but it had, at last, resulted in something positive.

Somewhere between darkness and dawn, she had finally come to the only conclusion possible.

She had to leave Grant and this place, and she could not let anything he said or did stop her.

There was no point in beating herself over the head for what had happened last night, or trying to figure out the reasons. It had happened, that was all, and it made no sense to keep playing the ugly scene over in her mind, telling herself that she should have slapped Grant's face or shouted for the housekeeper when neither thought had ever occurred to her.

That was the cold, humiliating truth. What she'd done was to turn to quicksilver in his arms, kiss him with a passion she hadn't known she'd possessed, and feel her body come to life under his touch. And if he hadn't put her from him . . . Crista took a shuddering breath. If he hadn't, she'd have ended up naked in his bed.

He'd probably tried to seduce her just to prove he could do it.

How she despised him! she thought as she closed the door to her room and started down the stairs. How she hated him, how—

"You're awake."

The cold voice made her start. Crista paused on the steps, her hand clutching the banister.

Grant was at the bottom of the stairs, looking up at her. His expression was remote, his gaze chill. It was a look at odds with the running shorts, sweatshirt, and sneakers he wore and with the faint, dark stubble that lay like a shadow across his unshaven face.

"It's a relief to know that you're so observant, Grant." She smiled, coolly, she hoped, although there was something in how he looked, that unexpected, raw male power that made her tremble. "Yes. I'm awake. And I want to talk to you."

Grant's gaze moved swiftly over Crista. She was wearing faded jeans and a pale lilac sweater that made her eyes look purple, and there didn't seem to be a hint of makeup on her face.

If he hadn't been feeling so grim, he'd have laughed. What would Zach say if he got a look at this *femme fatale*? She looked about as dangerous as a freshly plucked flower—which only made her all the more dangerous.

"Grant?" She made her way slowly down another few steps. "Did you hear what I said? We have to talk."

"I agree." He turned and made his way through the living room. Once out on the terrace, he swung toward her. "I've reached a decision," he said.

"So have I." Her eyes met his unflinchingly. "Either you remove yourself as my guardian or I'll contact Blackburn myself and demand it."

His mouth hardened. "Don't make threats, Crista. I don't like it."

"I don't give a damn what you like or dislike! I just told you something, and—"

"It's all taken care of."

She tried not to show any surprise, but it was impossible. She'd paced the night away in preparation for this moment and now there he stood, a smile playing across his lips as if to mock her.

Her tone was cautious and just short of belligerent.

"What do you mean, it's all taken care of?"

"I've decided to ask one of my partners to become your guardian." Grant picked up his coffee cup from the table, peered into it, and put it down again. "Sam is trustee for several of our clients, and—"

"Sam?"

"Samuel Abraham. He's a very capable gentleman in his sixties." A smug self-assurance crept into his tone. "And I promise you, if you try coming on to him the way you've come on to me, Sam will laugh you out of his office."

"The way *I* keep coming on to *you*?" Crista's eyes narrowed. "Is that the lie you whipped up for Blackburn?"

Grant sighed and leaned back against the railing.

"I didn't tell him anything, except that we've a compatibility problem."

"A compatibility problem." Crista's lip curled. "That's an interesting way to describe your behavior."

"*My* behavior?" A muscle knotted in his jaw. "No, my love. You're not going to make me the villain in this piece. Maybe I wasn't Sir Galahad—but you were far from the helpless maiden. Hell, you were as much a player in last night's little game as I was."

"That's a lie! I never wanted—"

"Didn't you?" He leaned away from the rail, his eyes locked on her face. "Shall I take you in my arms again so we can talk about who's lying and who's not?"

Crista's heart kicked against her ribs but her voice gave nothing away.

"This is a pointless conversation, considering that we've just agreed to remedy the situation."

After a moment, Grant nodded. "You're right. All that remains is to work out the details—and to deal with one final issue that's just come up."

Why was a warning bell going off in her head? And why was he looking at her that way?

Crista touched the tip of her tongue to her lips. "What 'final issue'?"

Grant looked steadily at her, then turned to lean his elbows on the railing and gaze out over the park.

"I just spoke with Horace Blackburn."

"You already told me that. You talked to him about resigning as my guardian."

"Actually, I didn't get the chance." He blew out his breath. "Are you aware that your uncle Simon owned an estate in Palm Beach?"

Crista's brow furrowed. "What do you mean, you didn't get the chance? Why not? And what does my uncle's winter house have to do with anything?"

Grant swung toward her. "Simon's house—I suppose it's an estate, really—is right on the water."

"Listen here, Grant, I'm sure this is all very informative but frankly—"

"But frankly, you're not interested in anything that doesn't concern you." Grant shot her a chill smile. "Well, this does concern you. Perhaps you've forgotten, but Simon's real estate belongs to you now."

"So?"

"So, Palm Beach was hit by a pretty bad storm during the night. It wasn't a hurricane, but the winds and rain packed quite a wallop."

"If you've something to tell me, do it and get it over with."

Hell, he thought grimly, that was just the problem. He did have something to tell her, and she wouldn't like it any better than he did. Damn, he thought wearily, damn, damn, damn!

"The bottom line is that the house sustained damage. Blackburn just got a phone call from the security people who patrol the place."

"And?"

"It seems a palm tree demolished the sun-room—and somebody's forty-two-foot cruiser is sitting in the middle of your back lawn."

"A pity," Crista said politely.

"The place is a mess. There's sand and glass and who in hell knows what inside. And there may be structural damage, too."

"So?"

"So," Grant said through his teeth, "it all has to be dealt with, and quickly."

Crista shrugged her shoulders. "Well, let the security firm take care of it. They can hire somebody to clean up, and to fix whatever needs fixing, and—"

"The security people are responsible for security, Crista, not for anything else."

"Well, then, tell Blackburn to call a cleaning service. Or a contractor. Or— Why are you shaking your head?"

"Blackburn's out of the loop. The will's been read, which means the property is your responsibility." His smile was grim. "And mine."

Crista felt a flicker of uneasiness. "I'm not following you, Grant."

"Someone in authority has to inspect the house and its contents, assess the amount of damage, determine what needs to be done and hire people to do the job."

Grant folded his arms over his chest. "Are you beginning to get the picture?"

Yes. She was—but she didn't want to.

"Come on, lady. You're not stupid. Must I spell it out for you?"

"Are you saying I have to do this myself?"

"Oh, not yourself," he said with an unpleasant smile. "Never by yourself, Crista." Grant's eyes narrowed. "I'll be right there, at your side, the way I'm supposed to be, offering my valuable experience and wise counsel."

Crista felt her throat constrict. "What are you talking about?"

"I'm talking about having to fly down to Palm Beach, dammit." Grant glowered at his wristwatch. "Blackburn's sending over the house keys by messenger, and—"

"No!" Crista shook her head wildly. "I refuse. It's out of the question!"

"I agree completely." His mouth thinned. "But I'm afraid we're stuck with each other for another day."

"That's crazy! This was Simon's house. It doesn't involve you."

"Until a court rules otherwise, I'm still your guardian, and responsible for decisions that concern your assets." Grant reached down and picked up his cup again. "That house is an asset. And any money spent on its repair or maintenance is subject to my approval."

Crista stared at him. Fly to Palm Beach? With Grant Landon? No. No! She'd have to be crazy.

"Then—then approve whatever needs doing over the phone. Talk to the security people. Or the police. What about an insurance agent? There must be—"

"There is. But I am not going to give a contractor carte blanche to cut a deal with an insurance company and then have to live with whatever they decide to do."

"I'd be satisfied with that," Crista said quickly.

"Only a fool would put herself in such a position."

"You said it's my property. And my money. If I'm willing—"

"But I'm not. How do I know you won't turn around a year from now and accuse me of allowing you to use your inheritance frivolously—or even fraudulently?"

Crista stared at him, her breath coming hard and fast.

"Tell me something," she said through her teeth. "Is it impossible for you to think anything good about anybody—or is it only me you hold in such low regard?"

"I'm only being prudent, Crista." His smile was quick and hard with disdain. "I know prudence isn't exactly a hypothesis you accept, but surely if you make the effort, you can understand the concept."

"Call this partner of yours, then. This—this Sam Whoever. He can fly down with me."

"Sam can't do anything, not until a court says he's legally responsible for you." Grant's mouth turned down. "Believe me, the thought of this little jaunt doesn't please me any more than it pleases you. Look, we'll fly in, reach whatever decisions must be reached, and fly back ASAP."

"As soon as possible is right," Crista said furiously. "I swear to you, Grant, I'd sooner go to—to the North Pole in a blizzard than to Palm Beach with you."

He laughed. "I couldn't have put it better myself."

He was still laughing as she turned and strode back into the living room, but suddenly his laughter faded and died.

He had a vision of Crista walking slowly toward him across a windswept beach. She was wearing a wisp of a bathing suit and her body was sun-kissed and hot as she came into his waiting arms. And when she lifted her face to his, her eyes were dark and filled with need...

Grant jerked the forgotten coffee cup to his lips and drank down all that remained of the black, bitter dregs.

Not that it would do any good, he thought.

It was going to take more than caffeine to get him through the next twenty-four hours.

CHAPTER SEVEN

CRISTA answered the light knock at her door to find Grant's housekeeper standing in the hall.

"Mr. Grant says to tell you your flight leaves in two hours, miss."

"Thank you, Mrs. Edison."

"He asks if you'd please be ready as soon as possible."

Crista smiled. She doubted that Grant's request had been made quite as politely.

"Of course."

"And he suggests you take only luggage you can carry on board, miss. He says—"

"He says," Grant's voice interrupted brusquely as he came striding down the hall, "that he's damned if he's going to stand around killing time at a luggage carousel."

Mrs. Edison's eyes widened as he brushed past both women. A second later, he was back.

"Do us both a favor, will you? Try leaving those miserable silver bells behind. The sound of them's beginning to drive me nuts!"

He vanished again. Seconds later, a door slammed farther down the hallway.

"Thank you, Mrs. Edison," Crista said calmly.

The housekeeper swallowed. "That's—that's quite all right, miss."

"You will take care of my cat for me, won't you?"

"Of course." The woman's face softened. "Don't you worry about a thing, Miss Crista. The one-eared fellow and I will get along just fine. You just go off to Florida and enjoy yourself."

Crista nodded, shut the door, and rolled her eyes to the ceiling.

Enjoy herself? On a trip she didn't want to take, to a place she didn't want to go, with a man she didn't want to be with?

She laughed mirthlessly as she opened her canvas carryall bag and began tossing things into it.

Oh yes, she was going to have an absolutely wonderful time. A marvelous time. A...

She paused, the sound of the housekeeper's voice echoing in her ears. How many "guests" of Grant's had the woman said those words to? How many other women had stayed here, in this apartment, and then gone off with him for a weekend?

They had not stayed in these rooms, she was certain of that. The women who'd come here before would have shared Grant's room and his bed.

But what did she care? What he did was none of her business, she reminded herself as she dumped her comb and brush into the carryall.

Any woman who could put up with Grant Landon was entitled to him. As for herself—she smiled grimly as she carefully took the silver-bell earrings from the dresser.

They annoyed him, did they? All the more reason to be sure to wear them, then.

It was the least she could do, considering that they were about to spend their last twenty-four hours together.

* * *

He was waiting for her in the entry foyer, and the sight of him was a surprise.

Crista had drawn her hair back into a French braid and tossed a denim jacket on over her jeans and cotton sweater, but other than that she was dressed as she had been during her confrontation with Grant on the terrace.

She'd expected him to disapprove of such casual attire, especially for a trip to posh Palm Beach, and that would be his problem, not hers.

But he was dressed very much as she was, in faded jeans that clung to his hips and legs more closely than she cared to notice, and he hadn't bothered shaving off that faint, sexy stubble.

His gaze swept over her without any sign of approval or disapproval, although he frowned when he spotted the earrings.

"Ready?" he said briskly.

She nodded, at the same time trying to ignore the sudden tightness in her throat.

It would have been better if he'd worn a suit and tie, if he'd shaved, if he'd done something to make it look as if they were going off on a business trip instead of it looking as if—as if...

"Let's get going, then. I want to get this damned trip done with as quickly as possible."

Crista's spine stiffened. "I couldn't agree more," she said, and swept past him into the elevator.

The first-class cabin was spacious and the seats wide. As soon as they'd reached cruising altitude, Grant slipped a portable computer from his briefcase and turned it on. Crista watched from the corner of her eye as his fingers began moving over the keyboard.

After a few moments, she sighed. Why hadn't she thought of taking along her sketch pad? Sketching would not just have made the time pass more easily, it would have relaxed her.

There was a yellow pad peeping out of Grant's briefcase. She waited a bit, frowned, then cleared her throat.

"Grant?"

"Yes?"

"Might I—could I use that notepad, please?"

He looked at her. "Why?"

Crista smiled tightly. "Because I want to use it."

"For what? There are magazines in the pocket in front of you, if you're bored."

"If I'd wanted to read, I'd have brought a book," she said testily. "May I borrow that pad or not?"

"I'll tell you what, Crista. I'll ring for the attendant. I'm sure she has a copy of today's paper."

Crista turned away and folded her arms across her breasts.

"Forget about it," she snapped.

"Dammit, must you always be difficult?"

"I'm not being 'difficult'. Believe it or not, I'm perfectly capable of finding ways to keep myself occupied without your assistance."

Grant glared at her and then he snatched the pad from his briefcase and dropped it in her lap.

"Take the damned pad. And a pen, too." His smile was swift and chill. "You can probably keep yourself amused for hours, making up lists of your boyfriends."

Crista looked at him. "Why, Grant," she purred, "you must be a mind reader."

Then she turned away sharply, tilted the pad at a comfortable angle, and set to work.

A long time later, she looked up, suddenly conscious of being watched.

It was Grant.

Lost in her drawing, she'd shifted toward the light coming in through the window so that she was almost leaning against him.

Crista flushed. "Sorry," she said. She drew back and started to tear off the page she'd been using but Grant stopped her, his hand closing on hers.

"What was that you were drawing?"

"It was nothing."

"It was a bird, wasn't it? But one I couldn't place."

Her flush deepened. "It was a phoenix."

"Ah. The mythological bird that's reborn in flame." He shifted in his seat so that he was looking at her. "I didn't know you drew."

"I don't," she said stiffly. "I design."

"Design?"

"Yes."

"What do you design?"

Her eyes met his. "Not boots," she said without a blink.

Grant's mouth quirked, and then, to her surprise, he laughed.

She sighed. "I design jewelry."

His brows lifted. "Jewelry?" His gaze flew to her earrings. "You mean—"

"Yes. These are mine. I do earrings mostly, and some necklaces and bracelets." She nodded toward the pad in her lap. "That would be the centerpiece of a necklace, but..."

"But?"

She looked at him. "I work mostly in sterling-silver wire. Bars of the stuff are too expensive."

"Not anymore," he said quietly, his hazel eyes on her face.

Crista smiled. "No. Not anymore. I keep forgetting that."

"So." Grant cleared his throat. "You have given some thought, then, to what you'll do with your inheritance."

Her smile tilted just fractionally. "Beyond spending it on boots, you mean?"

"Beyond spending it on your lover," he said, and instantly regretted it.

He saw Crista's eyes go flat, saw the slight but real smile disappear from her lips.

What had made him say something so stupid? Here they'd been having a conversation, a real one instead of their usual squabble...

But he was her guardian. It was his responsibility to keep her from doing foolish things. It wasn't the fact that she had a lover that bothered him; it was simply that it irked him to think of her squandering her inheritance.

"Crista," he said with a patient smile, "I didn't mean that the way it sounded."

"Yes, you did." She ripped the page off the notepad, balled it up, and jammed the pad into his midsection. "But that's okay, Grant." Her voice was frigid. "You've only got another—what?—twenty hours or so to criticize the way I live my life."

"I'm not criticizing. I'm simply trying to help you make the right decisions—"

Grant clamped his lips together. Crista had snatched the airline's glossy in-flight magazine from its pocket and now she was making a show of pretending to read it. She sure as hell wasn't listening to a word he said— not that he gave a damn. What did it matter if they managed a peaceful conversation or not?

He frowned and bent over his computer. But after a little while, he shut it off, stuffed it back into his briefcase, and spent rest of the flight looking out the window at the clouds.

Simon's house was on Ocean Boulevard, in the heart of Palm Beach.

Crista hadn't been sure what to expect. She had always been away at school when Simon spent time down here. But she'd seen pictures of Miami Beach, with what looked like traffic jams and endless hotels, all crowded together beside the blue-green sea.

At first, as their taxi sped them away from the airport, she thought this was going to be more of the same.

"You folks visiting for the first time?" the cabbie said, glancing in his mirror.

Crista looked at Grant. He was too busy glowering to answer. She sighed and looked back at the mirror.

"It's the first time for me," she said.

"Yeah, well, too bad you picked this time of year. The weather's not so hot, you know what I mean? But maybe you'll be lucky. The weatherman's not predicting anything much but some rain for the next day or so."

Crista craned her neck at a cluster of pale pink buildings as they rounded a corner.

"It's awfully crowded, isn't it?"

The cabbie chuckled. "Not where you're goin', it ain't."

It wasn't. Once they turned onto Ocean Boulevard, everything changed. They had entered a world that smelled of the sea, and the sand, and of luxury.

"That's the Kennedy place," the cabbie volunteered as they sped past a walled estate. "And that there is Mar-A-Lago. You know, the Trump joint?"

Crista had to smile. She had read about Mar-A-Lago. "Joint" seemed the wrong word for a Moorish mansion containing over a hundred rooms.

"And all the rest of these places?" she asked, leaning forward as she gazed out the window.

"Private getaways for the rich." The cabbie jerked his head toward an open iron gate that bisected a stone wall off to their right. "Like this place. You sure this is the one you're lookin' for?"

Grant spoke for the first time. "Quite sure," he said coldly, and the cabbie fell silent.

They drove up a long, straight driveway and stopped outside a massive, pink stucco house. Crista opened the car door and made her way slowly to the front door.

"My God," she murmured, "this place is huge!"

"And it's a mess." Grant grimaced as he looked around him. "There's the palm tree that came down. Hell, the window it took out looks like it's the size of a football field—and from what I can see, that's only half the damage."

He pulled the keys from his pocket, unlocked the door, and they stepped inside.

The tile floor was littered with glass and sand. Ahead, just visible in the sun-room, the downed palm lay like a fallen sentinel. It had taken a cabinet, a lamp, and half a sofa with it. Sunlight streamed into the room from the gaping hole in the ceiling. And beyond that, tilted on its side, a boat that seemed as big as the *QE2* sat in solitary splendor on the verdant back lawn.

"Oh my," Crista whispered.

"Oh hell," Grant said, and reached for the telephone.

Hours later, Grant shook hands with the last of half a dozen contractors, assured him that he'd be in touch as soon as he cleared his estimate with the insurance company, and shut the front door with a sigh of relief.

It had been a long, miserable afternoon. All he wanted now, he thought as he headed for the kitchen, was a bottle of cold ale—but he'd settle for a tall glass of anything with lots and lots of ice, followed by a cool shower.

The fallen tree had somehow wiped out the air-conditioning system, and he was hot and grimy from following more contractors through more cubbyholes and crawl spaces than he'd thought existed. He was irritable, too, tired of hearing one dire prediction after another of what would happen if he didn't get someone to make a dozen repairs within the next two minutes.

But mostly, he was royally fed up.

Crista had been at his side when the first contractor arrived, but somewhere between the roofer's musings and the electrician's dire warnings, she'd murmured something about the sun and the sand and vanished, leaving him to listen to the unending inventory of Things That Needed Fixing, which was a hell of an attitude to take when you considered that this was her house, not his. He would advise her on what to do, of course, but that didn't mean she didn't need to learn to bear responsibility.

Not that he was particularly surprised. Crista would always take the easy way out. She wouldn't think twice about leaving him to deal with the nitty-gritty while she explored the private beach behind the house and basked in the sun.

Grant frowned, turned a corner—and came to a dead stop.

Crista wasn't on the beach. She was in the kitchen instead, elbows deep in soapsuds at an enormous stainless-steel sink, wearing a cotton T-shirt damp with sweat and a pair of denim shorts.

He made a sound, something between a groan of despair and a whisper of surprise, and she whirled around, her eyes as wide and startled as a doe's.

"Grant!" She gave a laugh and lifted her arm, swiping her hair away from her forehead with the back of her hand. The T-shirt rose, exposing a band of ivory flesh at her waist. "I didn't hear you coming. Are the contractors gone?"

He swallowed dryly. "Yes."

"And? Is it as bad as it looks?"

"No. I mean, the house isn't about to fall down around our ears and the guy who owns the boat will remove it and pay for the damage to the seawall..." Grant cleared his throat. "What are you doing in here, Crista?"

Her eyebrows lifted. "What does it look like I'm doing? I've been trying to clean up. Didn't you notice that I'd swept most of the sand and glass out of the front room and the sun-room?"

He hadn't, but now that she mentioned it, nothing had crunched under his feet the past few times he'd walked through the place.

"I must have emptied a ton of sand out of here." She reached across the sink and shut off the water. "Now I'm doing what I can to salvage these little figures."

"Figures?" Grant echoed stupidly. "What figures?"

"These."

She plucked a tiny Dresden shepherdess from the sink and held it out, but the only figure he could seem to concentrate on was Crista's.

The damp T-shirt clung to her breasts, revealing their every detail. The shorts were ragged cutoffs. He'd seen skimpier ones on runners in Central Park, but all he could think about was that under them her legs were every bit as long as the boots had made them seem and her thighs were as golden and as rounded as he had dreamed.

In the distance, thunder rumbled across the ocean.

"There was a case filled with little porcelain statues near that broken window. I don't usually like fussy things like these but..." She gave a shrug and smiled at him. "They looked kind of dejected, lying toppled over, half-buried in a pile of sand. I thought I'd give them a bath—the ones that weren't broken anyway."

"I—I see."

"Lord, it's hot in here!"

He could see that for himself. Her face was flushed and her eyes bright; her French braid had come undone and strands of what looked like ebony silk curled lightly against her cheeks. As he watched, she lifted her hands to her hair and scooped it back behind her ears. The simple action made the tiny silver bells in her lobes tinkle softly—and made her breasts rise sweetly beneath her shirt.

Grant felt a pain wicked as a knife thrust twist inside his belly. He turned and yanked open the refrigerator door.

"I don't suppose there's anything cold to drink in this place," he growled.

"Just water. But I filled the ice-cube trays a while ago—they might have frozen by now." She stepped past him and reached for the freezer door. "Let me check—"

"I can check for myself," he said, catching his breath as her hip and shoulder brushed him with licks of flame.

"I don't mind." She laughed as she pulled out a tray and turned toward him. "Besides, it's wonderful, getting a blast of cold from that freezer." She gave an exaggerated shudder of delight. "I have to admit, I kept it open longer than I had to before, just so the cool air would do its job."

Don't look, Grant told himself, but it would have been easier not to have drawn breath. His gaze fell to her breasts.

Oh yes. Yes, the cool air had done its job this time, too. It had turned her nipples into buds, hard and visible under her shirt. He had only to reach out, to slide his hand over her...

Grant jammed his hands into his pockets and took a quick step back.

"Terrific," he snapped. "I was out there, sweating my guts out, listening to a load of gibberish and trying to make sensible decisions while you were in here, playing silly games."

"I was not playing games," she said carefully. "I told you, I was cleaning things. And—"

"And evading responsibility. I should have expected as much. Hell, the next time there's work to be done—"

The freezer door slammed shut with a bang. Crista spun toward him, her hands on her hips. The smile had faded from her lips and he told himself to stop, that she'd been working every bit as hard as he had and that he was making an ass of himself, but hell, it was safer doing that than—than . . .

He took a deep breath.

"Okay," he said.

Her head tilted. "Okay? Is that supposed to be an apology?"

"It's an admission that I'm too tired to quarrel. I need a cold ale and a hot shower and—"

"What you need," she said, waving her finger under his nose, "is somebody to call you the arrogant, self-centered ass you really are!"

"Look, I'm not in the mood for this. I told you, I want a shower and a drink and then I want—"

"Do you hear yourself? *You* want this, *you* want that! That's all you ever think of, Grant, what you want and what you think. Don't you ever get tired of being so damned selfish?"

"Selfish? Me?" He laughed. "Let me clue you in, lady. I have a law practice back in New York, in case you'd forgotten. And here I am in Palm Beach, in *your* house, dealing with *your* damages and *your* contractors, and for what?"

"I'll tell you for what!" Crista's face lifted in defiance. "For the joy of ordering me around. For the pleasure of—of playing lord of the manor with a bunch of men you're going to pay with *my* money to fix *my* house and you never even had the decency to turn to me and say, well, Crista, what do you think? Shall we ask Mr. Smith or Mr. Jones or Mr. Brown to patch that leak or—or fill that hole or—or fix the jousts—"

"Joists," Grant said with a smirk, "not 'jousts'."

"I don't care if it's joists or jousts or something midway between!" She stamped her foot with rage. "Just who in hell do you think you are!"

"Look, maybe we're both overreacting. I simply—"

"Simple? I'll tell you what's simple, Grant. It's your ability to be so sure you know everything there is to know about me."

"Crista, I know you're upset—"

"I'm not upset. I'm angry."

He could see that for himself. She was more than angry, she was enraged. Her cheeks were flushed, her eyes were dark. Everything about her sizzled with tension, and all at once he knew that that tension drew its strength not just from anger but from the same thing that was driving him, too.

"You're always criticizing me for what you think I've done or blaming me for what you think I'm about to do." Her mouth trembled. "Are you so perfect that you can afford to judge me?"

Grant took his hands out of his pockets. "I'm far from perfect," he said in a strained voice.

"Well, at least we agree on something!"

"If I were... hell, if I were..." He reached out and pulled her into his arms. "If I were perfect," he said, his voice harsh, "I wouldn't do this!"

He bent his head to hers and kissed her, hard, and just that quickly, she melted.

"Grant," she whispered, her voice soft and silky with desire. He groaned and took her lips again.

Lightning flashed at the window as rain began pelting the roof. And in the hot silence of that dusty room, time spun a slow web around them.

Her arms went around his neck, his went around her waist, and their mouths fused in passion. They moved from light into shadow, from the heat of the kitchen to the coolness of the long hallway, dancers caught up in the patterned steps of the oldest dance of all.

"Crista," Grant said, his voice thick and urgent. His hands cupped her cheeks, swept aside the silken strands of night black hair as he tilted her face to his. "My beautiful Crista."

He wanted to tell her more, to tell her that the feel of her body against his was almost more exciting than he could bear, that the smell of her skin was sweeter than any flower. He wanted to say her name again, over and over until it merged with the tinkling of the little silver bells that hung from her ears.

But most of all, he wanted to kiss her, to taste her and drink from her mouth, to savor the way she was kissing him back, her lips soft and warm under his, her tongue slipping against his with a delicacy that seemed unschooled.

His mouth clung to hers as he drew up her T-shirt and slid his hands over her back, her ribs. And when, at last, his hands cupped her breasts, she cried out his name and arched toward him.

"Grant," she whispered.

Did he hear the question in her voice?

If he did, he answered by kissing her more deeply.

It was no answer at all, and she knew it, but she would not, could not, stop him. Not now. Not ever. Not even if this was wrong.

How could she hate this man and want him at the same time?

And yet she did. She did.

His kisses were hot and scalded her mouth with desire. And his hands, the touch of his hands, the rough sweep of his thumbs across her nipples...

It was exquisite torture.

The girls at the restaurant had joked about this. They'd compared men, laughed openly at what it felt like to touch and be touched.

But she hadn't laughed. She hadn't known. She'd never dreamed a man's kisses, a man's touch, could do this.

Grant's kisses. Grant's touch.

She clung to him as he swung her into his arms and buried her face in his neck, inhaling his scent, tasting his skin with the tip of her tongue as he carried her up the stairs and into a bedroom.

Slowly, he laid her down on the silk coverlet and put his hand against her cheek.

"I want to make love to you, Crista."

A tremor went through her. "Yes," she whispered, and she covered his hand with hers and brought it to her lips.

Slowly, he stripped off the damp T-shirt that covered her, yet revealed so much. He looked at her breasts. They were high and perfect, the nipples dark pink against her creamy flesh.

"Beautiful," he said softly, and he cupped her breasts in his palms, stroked her nipples, and watched as her eyes closed with pleasure.

He bent, kissed the sweet rosebud peaks, drew them into his mouth. She trembled in his arms, his name on her lips, and finally he drew back, took her hands, and laid them against his chest.

Her fingers closed on his shirt buttons and undid them slowly. She slid her hand under the fabric and laid it against his skin, against the heat and hardness of his chest.

"Grant?" she whispered.

He looked into her face and caught his breath. Her eyes were dark, not just with need but with questions. With so many questions...

Crista shrieked as a chunk of plaster fell from the ceiling and smashed into the nightstand beside the bed. A drenching cascade of water poured from the ceiling.

Grant cursed, rolled to his side, and yanked her to her feet. "Hell," he muttered as he pulled off his shirt and draped it around Crista's shoulders.

She was soaked. Her hair hung in black rivulets and water dripped from the tip of her nose—and he knew he had never seen a woman more beautiful, or more desirable.

And he had no right to want her.

He was her guardian, sworn to protect her interests—which he'd done by telling her lies and half-truths, all so he could take her away from her lover. Or from her lovers. For all he knew, Crista Adams had slept with half of Greenwich Village.

It was a great combination, he thought bitterly. He had no ethics, she had no morals—and yet, he wanted

her anyway, wanted her so badly that he couldn't keep
his hands off her.

"Grant?" Crista hesitated. "The ceiling...
Shouldn't we—shouldn't we do something about it?"

He took a deep breath and forced his lips into a
smile.

"Of course. I'll go up there and see what I can do."

He turned away, wondering which was louder, the
rain drumming against the roof or the painful,
thudding beat of his own heart.

CHAPTER EIGHT

IT WAS still raining, and the wind roaring through the palm trees sounded like a freight train.

It was an awful night, Crista thought as she stared out her bedroom window, and she'd have given anything to be back in New York.

But they were trapped here. Grant had appointments in the morning and the storm had grounded all the planes...

What was there to worry about anyway?

She had faced the truth, and now she was free.

She sighed and let the curtains fall back into place. It wasn't original, but now she knew just how wise a thought it was.

This afternoon had been the end of whatever craziness had seized her the morning she'd stepped onto a curb and into Grant Landon's arms.

And she had the storm to thank for that.

What would have happened if the roof hadn't sprung a leak and a torrent of cold water hadn't come plummeting down on her head?

Crista's cheeks pinkened. She'd have ended up in bed with Grant, that's what would have happened. And heaven only knew how many lifetimes she'd have spent regretting it.

She shivered as she pulled a heavy cotton sweater down over her head. The temperature had dropped considerably since the afternoon; the house felt damp and chilled.

It would be a pleasure to get back to New York tomorrow, she thought as she tied the laces on her sneakers. Just a few hours from now, her life would be back on track, and Grant—Grant would be a question to be locked away, one she would never have to answer.

A shudder went through her again, and she frowned. What was wrong with her tonight? She couldn't seem to stop shaking.

A cup of coffee would help. And something to eat. Now that she thought about it, she hadn't had a mouthful of food the entire day.

Crista slipped open her door. She looked down the hall toward Grant's room. His door was firmly shut. She took a breath and made her way quietly down the stairs.

The kitchen was gloomy and old-fashioned, with dark wood cabinets, a noisy refrigerator, and an ancient gas stove. But there were still boxes and tins of food in the pantry, and that was all that mattered.

She turned on the lights and began putting together what she could for a makeshift meal. Olives and crackers. A box of angel-hair pasta and an unopened tin of olive oil. Tiny jars of dried garlic and porcini mushrooms.

And coffee. Definitely coffee.

A veritable feast, she thought, smiling.

Humming softly, she set to work.

Grant stood at his bedroom window, staring out at the storm and wondering what it was that fate had against him.

The weatherman—and the cabdriver—had predicted rain, but this stuff had as much relation to rain as the eruption of Krakatoa had to a campfire.

"Damn," he muttered, and dug his hands into the pockets of his jeans.

The storm was far offshore. That was what the radio kept saying, but for an offshore storm it was doing a great job of beating the hell out of this coastline— and an ever better job of trapping him here.

He'd tried everything to get a flight out, but not even a charter outfit would take off in this. So here he was, stuck in a house that looked like an overstuffed museum with a woman he couldn't seem to keep his hands off, and just for general effect, the wind was howling in the eaves like a banshee.

And he was hungry. Hell, he was starving! When had he eaten last? All he could remember was that pot of acid he'd brewed in place of breakfast and an airline lunch that he wouldn't have eaten under the best of circumstances....

And, heaven knew, nothing about this endless day had taken place under the best of circumstances.

Grant shuddered. It was like a refrigerator in here. Coffee, he thought as he pulled on a cable-knit sweater, that was what he needed. And a sandwich. There had to be something edible in that kitchen.

Halfway to the door, he hesitated. Did he really want to run the risk of bumping into Crista tonight?

"Stupid," he said under his breath, and he turned the knob and stepped briskly into the hall.

She was only a woman.

What on earth was there to be afraid of?

*   *   *

He heard her before he saw her. She was obviously in the kitchen and she was singing, softly and sweetly and vaguely off-key.

"...dah dee dah, and dah dee once again, it's been a dah, dah time..."

Grant paused in the arched doorway. She was standing at the stove, her hair loose and streaming down her back, stirring something with a big wooden spoon and swaying gently to the music as she built to a big finish.

"...a lonnng, lonnng tiiime!"

She swung around as he clapped his hands together. Surprise, and then embarrassment, flashed across her face.

"Must you do that?" she said.

He grinned. "I was only acknowledging a truly superior performance. It's not often you hear an old song sung so—creatively."

"You know what I mean. You shouldn't sneak up on people that way."

"I hate to disappoint you, Crista, but the only thing I was sneaking up on was my stomach. I got tired of listening to it growl."

She smiled a little. "Mine's been complaining, too."

He frowned as he came into the room. "What's that smell?"

"What's that smell?" She laughed. "It's garlic, of course."

"Garlic?"

"My God, don't tell me you've never heard of garlic!"

"Of course I've heard of it. I'm just surprised it smells so good."

She stared at him blankly. "You don't like garlic?"

Grant laughed. "Come on, Crista. You make it sound un-American. I promise, I like apple pie as much as the next guy."

"Well, anybody who loves apple pie should love this."

Grant peered over her shoulder. "This" was a mélange of golden and tan bits, sautéing in a skillet.

"What is it?"

"Sauce for the pasta in that colander. It's garlic and mushrooms and onion all browned together in olive oil."

He looked at her. "And it's good?"

"Good? It's delicious." She dipped the spoon into the pan and held it up to him. "Take a taste."

"I don't know..."

"Oh, come on. Be brave. Try a little."

He leaned forward and took a hesitant taste. Then he cocked his head, leaned forward again, and licked what remained from the spoon.

"Well?"

His eyes twinkled. "Not bad."

"Not bad?" She shook her head. "Delicious, is what you mean."

"It's okay."

"Come on, Grant. Just because it doesn't look like sushi—"

"I hate to disappoint you, but I hate sushi."

"Well, whatever's trendy, then."

Grant leaned back against the sink. "I think I've just been insulted," he said, his lips twitching.

Crista laughed. "Look, you're—what? Twenty-eight? Thirty?"

"Thirty-two," he said, still smiling.

"And you're a bachelor. And a New Yorker. And you're rich. That means—"

"That I eat raw fish?"

"It means you eat lots of nutritionally sound, incredibly expensive, basically tasteless things my mother wouldn't have let into her kitchen."

Grant laughed. "Don't tell me. Your mother was really Julia Child in disguise."

Crista reached past him for the pepper mill. A faint scent of violets drifted from her hair to his nostrils and he fought back the desire to reach out and touch his finger to the dark locks.

"My mother was half-Mexican." She glanced up at him with a sudden challenge in her eyes. "Did you know that?"

"No. But I suppose I should have guessed."

"Why?" Her chin tilted, more than matching the glint in her eyes.

Grant smiled. "The color of your hair for one thing. And your temper. They're both—"

"What?"

"Hey." Grant held up his hands in surrender. "What happened here? You were telling me that your mother was the Hispanic version of a master chef, and then, wham, you've got that look in your eye—"

"What look?"

"That one. The one that says you're spoiling for a fight." He tried not to smile. "I've come to recognize the signs."

Crista glared at him in silence and then she let out her breath.

"Sorry," she said, turning back to the stove. "It's just that—well, I suppose I'm a little touchy on the subject. My...lineage was a problem the past few years."

Grant's smile faded. "I don't understand."

"Uncle Simon," she said as she poured a thin stream of golden olive oil into the skillet.

"I still don't—"

"He never lost an opportunity to tell me that my father had married a woman who was—I think the kindest thing Simon ever called her was 'exotic'." Sighing, she dipped the spoon into the sauce, then lifted it to her nose, and took a sniff. "Mmm," she said. "It smells good."

Grant watched as she blew gently on the spoon. His body clenched as her lips parted; he saw the tip of her tongue and he turned away and took a deep, deep breath.

"It *is* good. Want another taste?"

He cleared his throat and looked at her.

"No," he said carefully, "no, I'll, ah, I'll pass."

She grinned. "Coward."

She bent toward the skillet again, lifting her hand to her hair and tucking it back behind her ear as she did. Her breasts rose gently beneath her sweater, and he almost groaned aloud.

Hell, she was right. He was a coward. Otherwise, he'd take her in his arms, claim her mouth with his, then carry her up to his bedroom, strip away her clothes, and finish what had been between them from the first minute they'd met...

"...worst food I'd ever eaten."

Grant swallowed. "I'm, ah, I'm sorry. I missed that."

"I said, when I went to live with my uncle, I couldn't believe the things his cook served." She was setting the table now, and she smiled at him over her shoulder. "Of course, Simon thought it was ambrosial. He said I was just being difficult when I didn't finish what was on my plate."

Grant forced himself to concentrate on what she was saying. "Sushi?"

Crista laughed. "You need a lesson in demographics. Simon was an old-line WASP of the worst kind. He believed in the restorative powers of vegetables cooked until they were limp and beef and chicken roasted until they were dry. Anything in a sauce was suspect." She gave a delicate shudder. "Meal after meal was the same. His cook gave a whole new meaning to the word 'predictable'."

Grant leaned back against the counter, his arms crossed.

"Predictable is bad?"

"Not necessarily. It's just that sometimes you need to try something different, something with—oh, I don't know. Something colorful."

"And if it turns out you don't like it?"

Crista laughed. "So what? You say yuck, that was awful. I hated it, I won't go near it ever again."

"I suppose you think that philosophy should apply to everything, not just to cooking," Grant said.

She looked at him in surprise. "I never thought about it, but—yes. I suppose I do."

His expression hardened. "That's a foolish way to live."

"Trying new things is foolish?"

"Dangerous, then. It's—it's..."

He frowned and clamped his lips together. When had this simple conversation gotten so complicated? And what the hell was he talking about? Crista was looking at him as if she thought he'd lost his mind, and he couldn't much blame her.

"Hell," he said, choking out a laugh, "I think I must be showing the effects of hunger on the human brain. Isn't that stuff ready yet?"

Crista looked at him a second longer and then she smiled.

"I think it is. Are you willing to risk my cooking?"

"Sure." Grant shot her a quick grin. "I can always go out the back door and catch myself some sushi on the hoof if I don't like the main course."

They smiled and settled opposite each other at the table and Crista watched as Grant took the first mouthful.

"Well?"

"It's good."

"Good?"

"Yes."

"Good?" she repeated, her eyes narrowing.

He laughed. "Okay. It's delicious. Does it have a name?"

Crista picked up her fork and twirled it through the steaming pasta on her plate.

"Uh-huh. Pasta with garlic and olive oil." She smiled. "I'm sure it does have a name, but I don't know it. I could..."

I could ask Danny, she'd almost said, and caught herself just in time. She didn't want to spoil this fragile peace. After all, they were parting tomorrow. Wouldn't it be nice to walk away from each other with a handshake instead of a grimace?

"You could what?" Grant asked.

On the other hand, she could tell him the truth. It was silly to let him go on thinking Danny was her lover.

"Crista? What were you going to say?"

No. It was none of his business what her relationship with Danny was. And besides, it seemed— it seemed safer tonight to let the deception continue...

"I was going to say that I could check my mother's recipes. She used to make something similar to this, except that her version had chili peppers in it."

"Chili peppers!"

She laughed. "Her Mexican heritage was incorrigible sometimes."

Grant looked at her. "You must have been devastated when your parents died," he said softly.

Crista's smile dimmed. "Yes. What made it even worse was Simon's determination to make me forget them."

"Forget your parents? But why—"

"Well, not my father. But my mother—that was a different story. 'I know you loved her, my dear Crista,' Simon would say, 'but now she is gone, and you must work to overcome that part of your ancestry.'"

Grant put down his fork. "Surely he didn't mean—"

"Of course he did. And I—well, I'd never run into that before. Growing up in the Village—"

"That's where you grew up? In Greenwich Village?"

She nodded. "Why do you look so surprised?"

"Well..." Grant frowned. "Blackburn said—he said..." He cleared his throat. "So. You weren't happy living with your uncle?"

Crista let out a sighing breath. "I tried to be grateful, to remember that he'd been under no obligation to take me in. But I didn't *want* to forget who I was. So I rebelled. Simon sent me to boarding school after boarding school. Each was supposed to make me sound and look like a lady, but I wouldn't cut my hair, or give up the way I dressed, or say what people wanted to hear instead of what I really believe."

"I see," Grant said quietly.

"So they'd send me back to Simon, who'd warn me that I was going to grow up to be just like my mother unless I mended my ways, and I'd tell him that was perfectly fine with me, and—and..."

Her eyes met Grant's and she flushed and shoved back her chair. "Just listen to me," she said as she snatched up their plates. "I don't know why I told you all this."

Grant stood up, too, and jammed his hands into his pockets. It was the only sure way he could think of to keep from walking to where she stood, putting his arms around her, and telling her that her uncle was a fool and that *she* was a fool for wasting herself on Danny. And Gus. And who knew how many others?

"Forgive me, Grant. I didn't mean to bore you to death."

Grant took a deep breath, then smiled.

"You didn't bore me," he said, "and, just for the record, good old Uncle Simon sounds like a prime ass."

Crista laughed. "Believe me, he was. And I never missed the chance to point it out to him. Subtly, of course."

Grant chuckled. "Of course."

"The only trouble was, it just reinforced what he already thought of me," she said as she filled the sink with soapy water. "I'd tell myself I was just playing into his hands, but—"

"But," Grant said as he took a towel from the rack, "you hated him so much that you could never resist the chance to nail him."

Crista looked at him in surprise. "How would you—"

"*Life With Father,*" he said with a tight smile. "My brothers and I all did whatever we could to rebel."

"You?" She shook her head. "I can't believe it."

"Do I strike you as such a straight-arrow, Crista?"

She looked up. His voice was suddenly soft and dangerous, and when she looked into his eyes, the images of what had happened between them in this room only hours before seemed mirrored in their depths.

"No," she said, dragging her eyes from his, "no, I didn't mean that. I just—I can't imagine you breaking the rules."

There was a silence. When Grant spoke again, his voice was harsh.

"We all did—Cade, and Zach, and me. Of course, we all did it differently."

Crista looked at him. "How did you do it?"

"Well, I was the eldest, so I was supposed to walk in the old man's footsteps. Be a football hero. Go to his university. And come home to work at Landon Enterprises."

"But?" she prompted softly, her eyes on his face.

"But, I went out for track instead of football, attended the university that was the longtime rival of his, and made my career in New York."

"Your father must have been furious."

He smiled tightly. "He said if I chose my own school and my own future, I could pay for it on my own, too."

"What did you do?"

Grant folded the towel neatly and hung it away. "I won a track scholarship to college, worked my tail off summers as a logger in northern Maine to pay for law school, and generally made it clear what my old man could do with his money."

"Ah," Crista said softly. "A self-made man."

He laughed. "Something like that."

"I'll bet your mother was proud of you, though."

His smile vanished. "My mother—"

He broke off in the middle of the sentence. My mother died before she should have, he'd almost said. She never knew what I did or didn't do with my life. And what would have made him say something like that, especially to this woman? As it was, he'd told Crista Adams more about himself in five minutes than he'd ever told anyone in a lifetime.

Well, that was what you got for being trapped in a mausoleum of a house with the rain beating down and the wind howling like something out of a bad horror film...

But it wasn't doing that anymore, he suddenly realized.

"It stopped," he said.

Crista blinked.

"What stopped?"

"The storm." He went to the back door and opened it wide. "Will you look at that? The moon is up." He turned to her and smiled. "Would you like to take a walk?"

It was such a simple question. Why was she so reluctant to answer? It was only a walk—a walk with Grant, along that dark, private beach, with the moon an ivory globe against the inky sky...

"Crista?"

He held out his hand, and she took it.

It was cool outside, and the air had the sharp, clean tang of the sea. Waves rolled heavily against the shore, the final, determined reminders of the storm.

Crista shivered slightly as they strolled along, and Grant put his arm around her shoulders.

"Cold?" he said.

She shook her head. "Only a little." She sighed. "Isn't it a beautiful night?"

Grant stopped walking and turned her gently toward him.

"Not as beautiful as you," he said softly.

The words were out before he could stop them. He hadn't meant to say anything like that; he'd only meant to take Crista for a walk along the beach. But all at once, he knew he needed more than that from her tonight.

Crista looked up at him. Was this the same man who'd spent the past few days barking out orders? It was as if he'd turned into someone else between the afternoon and the evening, a man whose smile was making her heart constrict within her chest.

It was a wonderful realization, but a terrifying one, too.

"Grant? Maybe we should—maybe—"

"Maybe we got off on the wrong foot."

Crista laughed. "Are we talking about my broken heel?"

"What if I were to put out my hand and say, 'Hello there, Miss Adams, my name is Grant Landon.'?"

"If you did—if you did, I'd say I thought it was time I cleared up some misconceptions."

"Misconceptions?"

"Yes." She took a breath. "Such as—such as—Gus."

Grant's smile tilted just a little. "I haven't asked you for any explanations, Crista."

"That's good," she said. Her smile was a little wooden. "Because I don't have to give you any."

"That's behind you anyway. Gus, and Danny, and—"

"That's what I'm trying to tell you, Grant. Gus was—"

"Wrong for you. I know. But—"

"Dammit," she snapped, shrugging free of his hands, "why in heaven's name did I think you'd changed? You're still a pompous jerk! Gus was my boss. My boss, do you understand? He owns the tavern where I waited tables. And—"

"You wore that rather interesting outfit to wait tables?"

"Yes! It's what gets you tips!"

"Let me get this straight. Am I supposed to be impressed because you got good tips?"

Crista glared at him. "No. No, you're not. I don't want to impress you. I don't even want to talk to you. I made the mistake of thinking you could be understanding, but—but you aren't even human! I promise, I won't forget it again."

Grant reached out his hand but she jerked away and started up the beach, away from the house.

"Crista! Come back here!"

She didn't turn around. Why had he ever thought he could carry on a conversation with this woman? And, dammit, why did he keep letting her work him into an obvious rage? No one had ever been able to do that, not until Crista Adams had come walking into his life.

"Crista!" His voice rose. "Crista—you're acting like a fool!"

She kept on walking, and he growled something sharp under his breath and started after her.

"Crista!"

What was she doing now? She'd come to a sudden stop, about a hundred feet away, and she was staring out to sea where waves as high as houses were building and crashing.

Grant frowned. There was something else out there—a tangle of storm-tossed debris and in its midst—in its midst...

A dog. A stupid, pathetic, doomed-to-death dog.

Grant's gaze swung quickly to Crista. "No," he said, and he began to run. "Crista, no!"

But he was too late. She was already racing across the sand, her hair flying out behind her, her feet sending up sprays of water as she hit the surf, and with his heart in his throat and her name on his lips, Grant pounded after her.

CHAPTER NINE

GRANT had been a runner almost his entire life.

He had run for the scholarship that freed him from his father's domination and for the glory of his school, but he had never run as hard or as fast as he ran now, with fear churning his blood and a desperate prayer on his lips, his eyes fixed not on some lofty prize but on something painfully real.

On Crista.

He could see her clearly in the moonlight. She was swimming strongly toward the dog, her strokes propelling her swiftly through the water.

But just beyond her, a wave was building, up and up until it looked like a wall of foam.

"Crista!" he shouted—but it was useless. She would never hear him, not with that wave roaring like a freight train as it came toward her. And even if she did, he knew she would never listen.

"Please," he whispered, "please, God..."

The surf churned around his ankles as he flung himself into the sea. The water was shockingly cold; he could feel it surge around him, and he kicked hard and struck out toward Crista, his powerful arms cleaving the night-black water just as the wave broke over her. Its waning edge caught him and tumbled him under. He broke the surface, gasping, straining to see.

There! There she was, ahead in the foaming water, a dark, struggling shape in her arms.

"Crista!"

She turned at the sound of his voice, though it seemed impossible she could hear him. Grant drew air into his lungs, buried his face in the water, and drove toward her.

Later, he would not remember how he got to her. He would only remember reaching for her, hanging on to her with a strength he hadn't known he possessed, telling her to let go of the dog, *demanding* she let go of it, and finally giving up any hope that she would.

"Hang on," he yelled, and together they struck out for shore.

When his feet finally touched bottom, he lurched forward, propelling her along with him. They fell forward, their faces in the sand.

Grant sat up, coughed out a mouthful of salt water, and clasped Crista's shoulders.

"Are you all right?"

She nodded while she struggled for air. Her face was a pale oval in the moonlight; her hair trailed down her shoulders like the ebony tendrils of some undersea flower.

"Yes," she gasped, "I'm okay."

The dog, still tightly clasped to her breast, shivered and gave a shrill yip. Crista hugged it closer and buried her face in its neck.

"Thank you," she said with a shaky smile.

Grant could feel every muscle in his body tighten. Did she have any idea how close she'd come to death? He had almost lost her. God, he'd almost—

A fiery mix of fear and rage surged through him, fueled by an unreasonably more volatile emotion.

"Damn you, Crista," he said through his teeth, and he yanked her to her feet, his hands coiled tightly around her arms. "What kind of a stunt was that?"

"What are you talking about?"

"You could have drowned out there!"

"But I didn't," she said, her smile dimming. "I'm a strong swimmer, and—"

"What you are is a self-centered, shortsighted fool! Don't you ever think before you act?"

"What was there to think about? The dog didn't have a chance."

"You could have died, dammit! We both could have!"

She pulled away from him, her spine stiffening. "I didn't ask for help."

"No, you didn't. What was I supposed to do? Watch you and that damned mutt drown?" He grabbed hold of her again and shook her. "Answer me, damn you!"

A convulsive shudder traveled the length of her body, leaving her drooping against him. Grant cursed and swung her into his arms.

"You don't have to carry me—"

"Next thing I know, you'll come down with pneumonia," he said as he strode across the sand and into the house.

"Nobody gets pneumonia from a midnight swim in Florida. You're making more out of this than it deserves."

Grant shouldered open the door to her bedroom and deposited her in the middle of the rug.

"Is that why your teeth are clicking like castanets?" He switched on the light and disappeared into the adjoining bathroom. When he emerged, she could hear the sound of water running. "I've turned the shower on. Go on now. Get out of that clothing and—dammit, Crista! Will you let go of that dog?"

"It's just a puppy," she said through the chattering of her teeth. "I have to dry it off."

"Dammit," Grant snarled, rolling his eyes to the ceiling. He marched back into the bathroom, came out with a stack of towels, and snatched the dog from her. "I'll dry the miserable thing while you get that clothing off."

"But—but you're soaked, too."

"Nice of you to notice, but at least my teeth aren't playing the rumba." When she didn't move, he glared at her. "So help me, get moving or I'll put this damned creature back where you found it."

Crista glared back at him, and then she stormed into the bathroom. The door slammed and Grant turned his attention to the shivering dog.

He dried it briskly and, in less time than he'd have imagined, it began wagging its tail and making playful feints at his hand.

"Feeling better, are you?"

The puppy yipped happily.

"You're wasting your efforts on me, dog." Grant scowled, crossed the room to a club chair, and arranged several dry towels on the cushioned seat. "As far as I'm concerned," he said as he placed the puppy in the improvised dog bed, "you're just one step up from her damned cat."

The puppy waggled its tail and delivered a sloppy kiss to Grant's hand.

"That won't keep me from being angry. Just thinking about what that headstrong, stupid woman did . . ."

The puppy curled into a tight ball, yawned, and fell instantly into untroubled sleep.

"That's it," Grant muttered. "Go to sleep. Why not? You've got nothing to worry about."

He watched the sleeping animal for a moment. Then, slowly, he knelt beside the chair and put out his hand. He hesitated, and then, very gently, he stroked his fingers over the soft, damp fur.

The dog would be dead now if not for Crista. What she'd done had been foolish, and risky, and crazy— and he could only hope he'd have done it himself if he'd seen the animal before—

"Grant?"

He shot to his feet and turned toward the sound of her voice.

She stood framed in the bathroom door, wearing a white terry-cloth robe that covered her from her throat to her toes. Her face was shiny and scrubbed, her hair was damp and loose—and with terrifying swiftness, Grant knew that it wasn't anger that had kept him going at all.

It had been fear—the fear of losing her, of never having had the chance to take her in his arms and make love to her, not in passion brought on by rage but in the sweet hunger of mutual desire.

"I thought you'd have gone to your room by now," she said.

He cleared his throat. "Yeah. Well, it took a while to get your pal settled in."

Her gaze flew to the puppy. "He's all right, then?"

"Yes." Lord! Here they were, having this foolishly mundane conversation about a dog, when all he wanted to do was go to her and take her in his arms...

"Yes, he's fine. How about you? How do you feel?"

She smiled. "I'm fine, too."

"No more chills?"

"No. The shower did the job." She seemed to hesitate. "Grant? I—I never thanked you."

"Yeah," he said briskly, "you did."

"No." She came toward him slowly, her eyes on his face. "I mean, I did try, down there on the beach, but you—you got me so angry that—"

"*I* got *you* angry?" Grant laughed. "Hey, *I* wasn't the loony who went dashing into that water."

He saw the smile slip from her face and he wanted to call back his words, but it was too late.

What was the matter with him anyway? What she'd done had been dangerous and impetuous—and wonderful. She was who she was; it was part of the reason he—he—

"You're absolutely right," she said woodenly. "I suppose if you'd been the one to spot the dog first, you'd have thought about it, analyzed it, probably demanded a case study of the situation, and by then—"

She gasped as Grant caught hold of her shoulders.

"If I were the coldhearted bum you claim I am," he said sharply, "you and that dog would be fish food."

"Listen, Grant, I'm grateful for what you did. But I told you, I'm a strong swimmer. I could have made that rescue without—"

"If I were a rational man, neither of us would be in Palm Beach!" His fingers dug into her flesh. "I'd have laughed myself sick the day Blackburn read us your uncle's will, turned around, and never looked back."

"I only wish!" Crista said, grimacing as she tried to free herself from his grasp.

"But I didn't do anything that sensible. Fool that I was, I let myself be drawn in."

"Well, you shouldn't have! You should have told Blackburn to find someone else to act as my guardian."

Grant's teeth showed in a cold smile. "I did."

Crista blinked. "You did?"

"Yes, dammit, I did. And Blackburn, that bastard, said he'd have himself named your guardian in my place."

"Well, why didn't you let him?"

Grant's mouth hardened. "Because I knew what he really wanted was to get you into his bed."

"And you could hardly have permitted that," she said with disdain.

"What sort of man would I have been if I had?"

"The sort who wanted to get me into his bed himself!"

She heard the rasp of Grant's indrawn breath, saw the sudden darkness fill his eyes. And she waited. Waited for him to explode with anger, to call her a liar...

Waited for him to gather her into his arms and crush her lips beneath his...

Crista's heart began to pound, not with fear but with a spiraling exhilaration.

"Grant," she said unsteadily, "Grant—"

She gasped as he let go of her and stepped back.

"You're right," he said in a harsh whisper. "And it's exactly the reason that tomorrow will be the last day we spend together."

He turned, and walked quickly from the room.

* * *

She fell asleep at last but she slept badly, slipping from one uneasy nightmare to another. Then, just before dawn, her eyes flew open.

Something had awakened her. A sound...?

She sat up, using both hands to lift her hair back from her face, and looked across the room. The puppy was still sleeping in his makeshift bed, her breathing deep and even.

What had she heard, then?

She swung her feet to the floor, pulled on the terry-cloth robe, and walked to the window, where she stood in the moonlight, looking out on the scene below.

The sea had calmed and become a black velvet canvas touched with sprays of white foam; the moon had waned and cast only a milky light on the deserted beach.

Crista's breath caught in her throat.

Grant was walking slowly along the surf as it lapped the sand—a tall, solitary figure wearing nothing but a pair of denim cutoffs. Moonlight spilled over his broad shoulders and leanly muscled torso; it streaked his dark hair with silver.

Tomorrow will be the last day we spend together...

A terrible sadness filled her heart.

"Grant," she whispered.

It was as if he'd heard her. He swung around and, before she could think or move, he lifted his head and looked at her. A thousand unspoken questions seemed to fly between them.

She saw his lips move. She knew he must be saying her name; despite the distance that separated them, she seemed to feel the whisper of it on her skin.

He took a step toward the house, his face still uplifted, his eyes fixed on her face, the tension in him almost palpable, and suddenly she gave a little cry, whirled around, and raced out of her room and down the stairs.

He met her at the foot, and his arms went around her in fierce embrace as hers circled his neck. Before she could speak, his mouth was crushing hers as she had dreamed it would, as she had prayed it would, and she breathed his name against his lips.

"Crista," he whispered, "my sweet Crista."

He swept her up into his arms and she clung to him while he carried her through the silent house, up the stairs and to his room. There, in an eddy of silver moonlight, he laid her down on his bed and undid the sash of her robe.

"How beautiful you are," he said as he drew the lapels of the robe apart.

She felt the sigh of his breath against her breasts, and then the warmth of his lips. She cried out when he drew back and slowly circled her nipple with his fingertip.

"Beautiful," he murmured, and he bent to her again and drew a waiting nub of flesh into his mouth.

The heat of his lips, the silkiness of his tongue, shot from her breast to her belly, coiled there like fire, then flamed out to heat her blood and melt her bones.

"Grant," she whispered with a desperate catch in her voice. She reached for him, but he caught her wrists and held them gently in one hand.

"Wait," he said softly. "Let me taste you and kiss you first. I've waited so long."

A soft cry broke from her lips as his hand moved between their bodies, over her belly and between her thighs.

"You're so hot," he whispered, "God, so hot and wet and ready for me."

Crista lifted her hips, moved blindly against his seeking hand.

"Yes," she said brokenly, "oh yes. Please, Grant, please ..."

He groaned, kissed her deeply, then rolled away from her and stripped off his denims.

"I can't wait," he said hoarsely. "Sweet Crista, I wanted to make this last forever, but—"

She had one sight of him as he loomed over her, his body beautiful and virile in the moonlight, and then she held up her arms.

"Now," she whispered, and he came down into her waiting embrace and, with one velvet thrust, made her his.

Hours later, a soft, early-morning breeze rustled the curtains.

Grant stirred and awakened slowly from a deep sleep.

He lay still, his eyes closed, trying to get his bearings. He was in a strange room, in a strange bed, and there was a woman in his arms.

And then he remembered.

He turned his head carefully and looked down at Crista. She was asleep, her dark head on his shoulder, her hand curled lightly against his chest. Her lips were slightly parted; he could hear the faintest whisper of her breath.

He felt an almost unbearable tightening in his throat.

How beautiful she was. Everything about her was perfect. He loved the way her long lashes lay against her cheeks, the way her hair cascaded over her bare shoulder. He loved the curve of her brow, the tiny indentation above her upper lip, and the line of her jaw.

She sighed in her sleep and snuggled closer to him, her hand opening against his chest. Carefully, so as not to wake her, Grant put his free hand over hers, smiling when her fingers instinctively laced with his.

It was going to be a perfect morning. The breeze was warm, the air sweet, and the early-morning light had the clarity of a fine Rembrandt. And he was lying in a wide, soft bed with Crista in his arms.

In his arms? Grant's smile tilted. That was a first. And she had surely been in his arms all these hours, now that he thought about it. His shoulder ached just a little, where her head lay against it.

Had he gone to sleep holding her? But he never did that after sex. Not that he was a thoughtless lover. On the contrary. He knew women liked to be held and he always obliged—but not to the point of discomfort. Besides, falling asleep with a woman in your arms was too intimate. More intimate, somehow, than the act of sex itself.

Grant frowned. The act of sex. What a way to describe what had happened in this bed. That instant when he'd first sheathed himself within Crista's satin flesh, her incredible tightness as she'd closed around him, her soft cry as she'd wrapped her arms around him and taken him deep inside her...

Just remembering made his body harden.

It might almost have been her first time. It wasn't, of course. He knew that. But if it had been, if he'd been Crista's first lover...

His frown became a scowl. Why in hell would he have wanted that? He wasn't a man given to scoring on virgins. Hell, no! If anything, he'd made it a point to avoid entanglements of that kind. He had no wish at all to become some wide-eyed innocent's romantic fixation.

And yet—and yet, he couldn't help thinking that it would have been wonderful to have been Crista's first lover, to have been the first man to have made her cry out beneath him, the first to have made her whisper "yes, oh yes, oh please..."

"Dammit," he said, muttering the word softly from between his teeth.

Carefully, he eased his arm from beneath her head and sat up.

What was the matter with him this morning? He'd slept with Crista and it had been terrific. It had been incredible.

But sex was all it was.

The old song said it best. Birds did it. Bees did it. And he did it—heaven knew he'd bedded enough beautiful women in his life and, if they were to be believed, none of them had left his bed unsatisfied.

He was, with all due modesty, a man who understood the pleasures to be found in sexual passion without ever being foolish enough to wax poetic about them.

So why was he sitting here, spinning drifts of purple prose in his head?

Why could he remember each touch, each whisper? Why did he ache with wanting to kiss Crista awake and then make slow, heated love to her again? There was no logical reason for it...

Maybe there was. His liaison with Crista had not been illegal but it had certainly been immoral. He'd violated his own code of ethics last night. That was why what had happened had seemed so special—because it had been wrong.

Forbidden fruit was always sure to taste sweeter.

Suddenly, the warm air seemed uncomfortably humid, the scent of the sea acrid and unpleasant. Grant rose, glanced at his watch as he put it on, and stepped into his denim cutoffs. He zipped the fly, then walked slowly to the window.

It would have been better not to have given in to temptation and slept with her, but he wasn't a man to waste time on regrets. The thing to do now was put the mistake behind him. He had a couple of appointments this morning, but nothing that wouldn't be finished in plenty of time for them to catch their return flight to New York. By this evening, Crista would be in Sam Abraham's charge. And this time in his life would be history.

He felt as if a weight were lifting from his shoulders as he looked out at the sea. It was calm again, and the sun was a bright yellow disk in the cloudless blue sky.

Everything was back to normal—and so was he.

Crista lay in the bed, watching as the morning sunlight lit Grant's stern profile.

A moment ago, she'd awakened to a feeling of such happiness that she'd almost flung herself from the bed and raced across the room to where he stood. But then she'd seen the tension in his shoulders, the look of cool disapproval on his lips, and the joy in her heart had died.

It didn't take any great effort to figure out what he was thinking. He'd wanted to make love to her from day one, but he'd fought against it.

Now he was regretting last night's lapse, and trying to figure out how to handle what might be a potentially disastrous "morning after".

A lump rose in her throat. It had all seemed to be perfect. Nothing she'd ever read or heard or even dreamed had prepared her for such joy. The happiness she'd found in Grant's arms had been indescribable, not just when they'd made love but even when he'd simply held her close, kissed her gently, and whispered of the pleasure she gave him.

Had it all been an illusion?

Maybe—maybe she was misreading the signs. She was embarrassingly new to this. How did she know what to expect from a man who'd just made love to a woman for the first time? Grant was simply standing at the window, staring out to sea. For all she knew, his thoughts were a million miles away. He could be thinking about a business deal back in New York, or all the work that needed doing on this house, or the appointments he had scheduled this morning.

She took a breath, sat up quietly, and wrapped the sheet around herself. Then she rose from the bed and started toward the window and Grant, but he turned toward her before she'd gone half the distance.

"Good morning," he said. His tone, and his smile, were the polite ones people give strangers.

"Good morning," she replied. Silence stretched between them. "What—what time is it anyway?"

Grant looked at his watch, then at her. "Almost seven."

"Ah." She nodded foolishly. "Almost seven. I thought it was later."

Silence engulfed them again, and then Grant cleared his throat.

"Did you sleep well?"

"Oh yes," Crista said, "yes, I slept like a log. It must have been..." Her cheeks colored. "It must have been the sea air."

"Yes. I suppose it was." A faint furrow appeared between his eyes. "Crista. About last night..."

She looked at him and she waited, and, at last, she knew she had to face the truth.

"Yes," she said, her head high, "about that, Grant. It was—it was—"

"It was—terrific."

"Terrific," she said, and shot him a bright smile. "Exactly. But—but—"

"But it was a mistake. My mistake entirely." His mouth narrowed. "I know an apology is useless, but—"

"Please. Don't—don't apologize. What happened was—it was just one of those things. And—and—"

"And now we can get on with other things," he said briskly. "Our business here, and then our flight back to New York—"

"Good. Good." Horrified, she felt a sudden constriction in her throat. "I, ah, I think I'd like to take a shower, if you—"

"Of course." Grant moved quickly to the door, obviously every bit as eager as she to end this uncomfortable scene. "I'll, ah, I'll start the coffee."

Crista nodded. "Fine."

"I'm not very good at coffee." His smile was quick and overly bright. "I suppose you learned that yesterday morning, but—"

"For God's sake, Grant! Just—just go on and get out of here, will you? Let me—let me..." She stared at him in dismay, then took a shuddering breath. "I'm sorry," she whispered. "I wanted to make this easy, but—"

"Crista..."

She shook her head wildly, hating herself for such a pathetic show of weakness, hating him for the pity she saw in his eyes.

"Please, Grant. Don't say anything. Just—just go."

He hesitated, but finally he did as she'd asked. As soon as the door closed, she groaned and flung herself across the bed.

What had made her behave like such an awful fool? So she'd slept with Grant. So what? The world was filled with women who slept with men; one night together didn't mean—didn't mean—

The door banged open.

"Dammit to hell," Grant roared.

Crista rolled over and sat up, clutching the sheet to her chin.

"Grant, what's the matter? Is it the roof? The seawall? Is it—"

He came down on the bed beside her, gathered her close in his arms, and kissed her long and hard. She resisted at first but then, with a sob, she threw her arms around him and gave herself up to the kiss.

It was Grant who ended it, drawing back and framing her tearstained face in his hands.

"It's bad enough that I'm a liar," he said gruffly, "saying that making love with you was terrific when it was so much more than that, when it was like nothing I've ever known. But to go on and behave like a complete fool..." He paused and took a breath. "I don't want to go back to New York, Crista. I want to stay here and make love under the heat of the sun, swim in the moonlight..."

A smile trembled on her lips. "Do you mean it?"

"And when we get back to New York, you won't need Sam to look out for you because you'll have me."

"Oh, Grant—" A shrill bark made them both start. Crista wiped her eyes and laughed. "The puppy! I forgot all about—"

"Yeah." Grant sighed and dropped a kiss on her forehead. "I suppose we'd better see what it wants."

"What *she* wants." Crista smiled. "And that's easy to figure out. She wants a meal, a walk, and a scratch behind the ears."

Grant smiled, too, but as he watched Crista hurry off to tend to the dog, his smile faded.

Moments ago, he'd come bursting back into the room, filled with the knowledge that he could not let Crista walk out of his life.

The puppy barked again, and he sighed.

The dog knew what it wanted—but what did *he* want, Grant wondered, of himself and of Crista? If only it were as simple to figure that out...

Lord, if only it were.

CHAPTER TEN

THE sun was hot, the sky was the color of sapphires, and the sand glinted as if it had been shot through with diamonds. Crista and Grant came pounding toward the house side by side, the puppy racing after them at the end of an improvised rope leash.

"I win," Grant yelled.

"No, you don't!" Crista gave a wild whoop, clipped him with an elbow—and then the puppy darted between them and they both went down in a heap.

Grant gave a dramatic groan and flopped onto his back, his eyes shut.

"No fair," he said. "You bribed the dog so it would do that."

Crista rolled onto her belly and lay spread-eagled in the sand.

"Why would I resort to bribery?" she panted. "I was winning."

"Impossible." Grant opened one eye and looked at her. "I'm the best, and I've got a drawer full of medals at home to prove it."

"Yeah, yeah. The bigger they talk, the harder they fall."

She shrieked as he caught her in his arms and rolled her beneath him.

"Watch the way you talk to me, madam, or I won't be responsible for my actions."

"Promises," Crista said, rolling her eyes. "All the man makes are prom—"

161

Grant silenced her with a long, deep kiss.

"When was the last time I told you how beautiful you are?" he whispered when the kiss ended.

"Probably the last time I told you how beautiful *you* are."

He laughed. "Men aren't beautiful."

"Says who?"

"Says—hey!" Grant laughed as the puppy began tugging at his shorts and growling. "What's with you, monster?"

Crista smiled. "She wants to play."

"Okay, pal." Grant scrambled to his feet and the puppy yipped with joy. "You wanna play rough? We'll play rough!"

Smiling, Crista watched as man and dog settled into a fierce game of feint and run, and then, slowly, her smile faded away.

The past days had been so wonderful—it was hard to think that they'd be back in New York tomorrow evening. But there was no choice. Grant had already put off a week's worth of appointments.

She sighed and flung her arm over her eyes. Returning to New York was something that had been bound to happen eventually. It was just that she had an awful feeling that nothing would ever be the same once they were back in the real world.

Palm Beach, after all, was not reality. It was magic. It was where she'd discovered passion, and happiness, and Grant.

Grant, she thought with a little sigh. What a complex man he was. He could make friends with the puppy by getting down on his knees in a game of mock combat as easily as he could bring to heel a sommelier brandishing a wine list whose primary function in life was surely intimidation. He was, by turns, funny and warm and wise...

He was, in other words, the man she'd sensed him to be all along—and the man she'd fallen in love with.

Crista sighed, rose to her feet, and made her way slowly into the house. It was cool and dark after the bright, sunlit beach; she shivered slightly as she climbed the steps to the bedroom she and Grant shared and paused in the doorway. There was something about seeing the bed that put a lump in her throat. They had shared so many nights there together and now—now, it was all coming to an end.

No! Why did she keep thinking things like that? They were going back to New York tomorrow, that was all. Nothing else would change, she reminded herself as she took off her bathing suit and stepped into the shower. Grant wanted her to be with him, he'd talked about the places they'd go in the city and the things they'd see....

But he'd never said he loved her, that he could not imagine a future without her as she could not imagine one without him...

She gasped as the door to the shower stall opened.

"Excuse me, madam," Grant said politely. "I was wondering if you'd mind practicing water conservation and sharing that shower with me."

Crista laughed and thought how glad she was that the water would hide the dampness that glittered in her eyes.

"I don't know, sir," she said. "I'm not sure there's room for two."

He stepped under the spray and took her in his arms. His body was hot from the sun, hard with masculine power, and she felt herself quicken when he touched her.

I love you, Grant, she thought.

And then she couldn't think anything at all.

Grant watched as Crista puttered around the kitchen. She was barefoot, dressed in shorts and a cotton shirt. Her hair was a dark plume that tumbled down her back, her forehead was red, and she had a gob of white zinc oxide on her nose.

He smiled. In other words, she was gorgeous. And she was his.

He had never known a woman like her, a creature of ardor, fervor, and pure emotion. The other morning, he'd found her sitting on the floor with the puppy in her arms, sobbing. And when he'd come down quickly beside her and asked her why, she'd said, laughing and crying at the same time, that it was because she'd just thought again of how the little dog might have died.

And then there was last night, when he'd asked her how she liked the vintage burgundy he'd chosen for their dinner, and she'd laughed and said, well, it tasted better than the jug wine she was used to—but not by much.

That had brought a smile even to the thin lips of the haughty sommelier.

Actually, she'd brought smiles to lots of lips last night. They'd dined at one of Palm Beach's most prestigious restaurants. The season had not yet really begun but the candle-lit tables had been crowded with exquisite women dressed in their Chanels and Armanis, their hair sleeked back from their artfully made-up faces, their jewelry elegantly discreet.

Crista had worn a halter-necked drift of bright coral silk she'd bought during an afternoon stroll along exclusive Worth Avenue. Her hair hung free over her tanned shoulders and cascades of tiny silver leaves swayed from her earlobes. Circlets of the leaves clung to her wrist, and her only makeup had been the blush put in her cheeks by an afternoon spent in Grant's arms.

The women in the place had cast her discreet looks, equal parts amusement and envy. But the men's glances had been filled with admiration, and Grant had had all he could do to keep from leaping to his feet and shouting that Crista Adams, this untamed, magnificent wildflower blazing in a pallid sea of greenhouse blossoms, belonged to him . . .

"Whatever you're thinking about, I'd bet it has nothing to do with the tuna fish I asked for."

Grant looked up. Crista was smiling at him teasingly, and he smiled back.

"Sorry, darling. I must have been daydreaming. Tuna, did you say?"

"Please. I think we bought some, didn't we?"

Grant supposed they had. He'd wanted to hire a housekeeper for the week, but Crista had insisted that shopping and cooking and keeping the house clean would be fun. And, to his amazement, she'd been right. He'd never had the time or the desire to learn to cook—his law practice had taken all his energies—and he was no master chef now, he thought as he handed over the tuna, but this past week, he'd learned that grilling a steak on an outdoor grill could be fun.

"Here," Crista said, "you slice the tomatoes and tear up the lettuce. I'll do the rest."

Not that Mrs. Edison was in danger of losing her job, he thought with a little smile. And yet, things would surely change once they got back to New York. Things would change in both their lives.

Grant's smile faded. The business about Danny, for instance. They hadn't discussed that yet, but they would. He had to know more about that, had to know if Danny had really mattered to her, if anyone before him had mattered....

"Grant?" He looked up. Crista was watching him, a hesitant smile on her lips. "Is everything all right?"

He put down the tomato and the knife and took her in his arms.

"It's never been better."

It was true, he thought as he kissed her. For the first time in his life, he was truly, completely happy—and yet, deep inside him, he sensed a whisper of unease.

That night, Crista announced that she'd named the dog Annie.

"Short for Anonymous?"

"Short for Orphan Annie," she said as they strolled the beach, hand in hand. "I don't think the poor baby ever had a real owner. Isn't she a cute puppy?"

Grant looked at the dog, trotting nose to the sand ahead of them. Either it was at some gawky adolescent stage, with feet and ears too big for its body and a muzzle that seemed all whiskers, or it was among the homeliest creatures he'd ever seen.

"Cute's the word, all right," he said.

"She needs a collar and a real leash, Grant, and—"

"Crista," he said gently, "it—she—can't go back to New York with us. You know that, don't you?"

"But if I'm right, if she has no home—"

"I'll look in the phone directory and see if there's a dog warden, and—"

"The shelter in the Village would take her, Grant. They'd be able to find her a good home."

"Shelter?" Grant's brows lifted. "What shelter?"

"The Good Shepherd Shelter. They're wonderful about finding homes for strays."

Grant sighed. "Look, I don't mean to be difficult. But transporting an animal is—"

"A cinch!" She swung toward him, her eyes wide. "I've read lots of articles about it. The airline has crates you can buy. It's not a problem at all."

"But—" He looked at her, at the hope in her face, and he sighed. "You're sure the shelter will accept her?" Crista nodded, and he drew her into his arms. "You're corrupting me, woman," he said sternly. "First I cancel all my appointments for the week, then I agree to play foster parent to a mangy mutt. What's next?"

She moved closer into his embrace. "I can't imagine," she whispered. "Suppose you tell me."

And, in soft, sexy words that made her blush, Grant did.

They left Palm Beach in late afternoon, taking off into a bright, cloudless sky. They landed at Kennedy Airport three hours later in a cold, gray downpour.

Grant took Crista's elbow and started toward the terminal exit door, but she shook her head and hung back.

"We can't leave yet."

"Why not?"

"We have to get Annie." She smiled and looped her arm through his. "We have to wait until her kennel's unloaded."

Grant frowned. "I'd forgotten."

"The sooner we get to the baggage area, the sooner we can collect her and leave."

It was half an hour before they finally climbed into Grant's waiting Mercedes and an hour after that, thanks to the rain and the traffic, before they were in his private elevator.

Grant felt his stomach knot as the car rose toward the penthouse floor. He had felt strangely tense all during the flight home. Now, that tension was growing and he knew the reason.

He had left here determined to walk away from Crista Adams, and returned with her as his lover.

The realization hit home with almost physical force. He was bringing her back to stay, not because he felt responsible for her but because he felt—he felt—

What *did* he feel? The knot inside him tightened and made it hard to breathe. He turned to Crista, needing to take her in his arms, to kiss her...

But it was too late. The doors slid open and she gave a little cry, dropped to her knees, and opened her arms to a hurtling gray shape.

"Hello, Sweetness," she said happily. "I missed you, too."

Grant watched the woman and the cat, his face expressionless. Then he reached down for his overnight bag and hers and strode briskly toward the staircase.

*   *   *

The next day did not begin well. The rain had stopped, but the sky was overcast. And Grant awoke to an empty bed.

Showered, shaved, and dressed, he made his way downstairs.

Crista was in the living room. She was seated on one of the white leather sofas, wearing a hot pink sweater over purple leggings. Her hair was loose and lay in soft disarray over her shoulders, and the silver-bell earrings dangled from her earlobes.

Back in Palm Beach, she'd worn this same outfit and looked heart-stoppingly beautiful. She still looked beautiful—but as out of place against the pristine white elegance of the room as the beaten-up cat beside her or the happily grinning dog at her feet.

Grant could feel that knot forming in his belly again.

"Grant!" Crista leaped to her feet and came toward him. "Good morning! I didn't hear—"

"I thought we agreed the cat would be confined to the guest room."

"I know we did, but that was before—"

"The change in our relationship hasn't changed my feelings about cats, Crista."

Her face whitened. "I meant before Annie came along. I'll have to keep them locked up together until the shelter takes her, and I wanted to give them the chance to get to know each other. If you think I was trying to presume on what's happened between us—"

"Damn!" He covered the distance that separated them in two long strides and took her in his arms. "I'm sorry, darling. It's just that—well, I'm running late and..." He laughed, hoping she'd laugh, too, but she didn't. "I guess mornings aren't my best time. Which reminds me—where were you when I woke up?"

He felt the tension begin to go out of her. "Did you miss me?"

"You're darned right, I missed you. Where'd you go?"

Crista gave him a slow, mysterious smile. "Well, I knew you'd given Mrs. Edison the week off and that she isn't due back until tomorrow, so I made you breakfast."

"Breakfast?" He looked past her to the terrace, where the table had been set. "That was sweet, darling, but—"

"You know those pecan waffles I made in Palm Beach, the ones you liked so much?" She took his hand and began to tug him toward the door. "I couldn't find any pecans, but I did find chocolate chips, and—"

"Chocolate chips? In waffles?"

She laughed. "Come on, Grant. You didn't think you'd like garlic either, remember?" Her fingers laced through his. "There's fresh orange juice, too, and coffee, and—"

"I never eat breakfast."

"Sure you do. You ate it every day in—"

"That was different," he said more sharply than he'd intended. "Palm Beach was a different world, Crista—" He stopped, hating himself when he saw the hurt in her violet eyes. "What I mean is that Mrs. Edison's been cooking for me for years. We wouldn't want to upset her, would we?"

"No. Of course not, but—"

"Damn!" Grant frowned at his watch. "I've a meeting at nine."

"Grant? I wanted to talk to you about—"

"We'll talk tonight," he said as he walked quickly toward the foyer with Crista hurrying after him. "Oh hell. I've got to go out tonight."

"Tonight? It's our first night back."

"It's a charity ball at the Waldorf. We won't have to stay all evening."

"But I hate things like that. Can't you just send in a contribution and stay home?"

"My firm's bought a table, Crista. It's only right I make an appearance."

"But—"

"Dammit, I can't stand here and argue." Grant stepped into the elevator car. "Buy yourself a gown at Saks," he said as the doors slid shut. "I'll see you at six."

Crista stood staring at the closed car doors. After a moment, she swallowed hard and turned away.

Had Palm Beach been magic—or a mistake?

In the elevator, Grant leaned back against the wall, the frozen smile slipping from his face as he wondered the very same thing.

Filled with contrition, Grant came home at five instead of six. All day long, he'd heard his own stuffy voice echoing in his head. What in hell was the matter with him? A stupid charity ball was nowhere near as important as Crista, and he'd canceled his last meeting of the day so he could get home early and tell her that in person—but he needn't have bothered.

The apartment was empty except for the cat and dog meowing and barking in the guest suite.

At 5:15, he scoured the rooms to see if he'd overlooked a note.

At 5:30, he picked up the service phone and asked the doorman if he'd seen Miss Adams go out.

At 5:45, he went through a mental list of the things that could happen to a woman on the streets of the city.

At 6:00, he told himself it was too soon to call the police.

And at 6:15, the elevator doors opened and Crista came flying into the foyer.

"Grant," she said with a little laugh, "you're home!"

He looked at her. Her face was flushed, her eyes bright, her hair in disarray, and an awful coldness seized his heart.

"Indeed." He folded his arms against his chest. "That's certainly more than can be said of you."

"Oh, I know. And I'm sorry, but—"

"Where were you?"

"Downtown. The time just got away from me, and—"

"I thought you were going to spend the day shopping."

"You were the one who said that, not me." She frowned and took a step toward him. "Grant? What's the matter?"

"Nothing. Nothing's the matter." He glared at her. "It's after six, we have to be out of here in an hour, and you—you look as if you spent the day in bed!"

He wanted to call the words back as soon as he'd said them—and yet, he was glad he had. What did he know about her? Only what she'd chosen to tell him— but Blackburn had told him other things.

"You know," Crista said, her lips trembling, "I've played this scene before."

"Come on, Crista, don't avoid the issue. I want to know where you were."

"My uncle used to leave for his office in the mornings after giving me my instructions for the day, too. Sometimes, he'd even tell me to go to Saks, just as you did." She lifted her chin and forced a smile to her lips. "It was a polite way of telling me to buy myself something ladylike."

"I never said—"

"And, at night, he'd give me the third degree, the same as you. Well, I'll make it easy for you, Grant. I'll tell you exactly where I was." Her eyes blazed with defiance. "I was in the Village."

"With Danny," he said, his hands knotting at his sides.

"Is that what you think?"

"I don't know what I think, dammit! That's why I'm asking you!"

"No. You're not asking me. You're accusing me."

Grant stared at her. He wanted to storm across the floor, take her in his arms, kiss her, shake her, something, anything, until she told him that she didn't give a damn for Danny or for any other man, that she only wanted—only wanted—

He took a step back and jammed his hands into his pockets.

"If we're going to be out of here by seven," he said coldly, "we'd better get started."

Crista looked at him for a long moment, and then she let out her breath.

"All right," she said. "I'll go and take my shower."

Twenty-four hours ago—a lifetime ago—he'd have smiled and said he'd take that shower with her.

Now, he only clamped his lips together and turned away.

The ballroom at the Waldorf was thick with famous faces and famous names. Under other circumstances, all the air-kissing as well-groomed cheek met well-groomed cheek would have made Crista smile.

Tonight, it only made her feel like an anthropologist watching some strange tribal ritual.

Grant was not doing any kissing. He wasn't doing anything. He was just sitting at her side as silent and cold as a tomb.

They were at a table for ten, five men in dark dinner suits, four women in the pale beige that was the designer color of the season—and Crista.

They were all dying to know who she was, she could tell. Grant had introduced her, of course, but after that, he'd lapsed into his stony silence. Now, everybody at the table was trying hard to pretend nothing was wrong when, in reality, they all knew that something certainly was.

Crista felt uncomfortable and—for the first time in her life—painfully conspicuous. She'd planned to do as Grant had asked, go to Saks and buy their simplest, quietest, most elegant Givenchy or Chanel, if that was what it would take to make Grant smile at her again as he had in Palm Beach.

But there hadn't been time. She had spent the day going in what had seemed like a million different directions, from a guilty stop at the soup kitchen to help prepare lunch to a meeting at the animal shelter, where she'd arranged for Annie to be taken in even though parting with the dog would break her heart. While she was there, one of the attendants had fallen ill and she'd ended up cleaning out kennels. Last but most importantly, she'd stopped off at her apartment to tell Danny that he could stop worrying about her, that she was happy and in love...

Which was why she'd ended up not cool and proper in a designer original but looking like a neon sign in the gown she'd bought in Palm Beach, and—

"Do you want to dance?"

Crista looked up. Grant was leaning toward her, smiling politely although his eyes were still cold and angry.

She nodded. Anything was better than sitting here and pretending to give a damn about Muffy's latest trip to the Côte d'Azur.

She went into his arms as soon as they reached the dance floor. He held her stiffly, but gradually the music softened and so did Grant's embrace.

"I'm sorry," he whispered.

Crista felt tears spring into her eyes. "Oh, Grant, I'm sorry, too."

"I had no right to accuse you of..."

Grant's apology stumbled to a halt. It was like being out with her in Palm Beach. People were staring.

"It was my fault," she whispered. "I should have been home on time."

He cleared his throat. "No. I had no right to—"

Hell! People were staring, but men were gaping. There was a man at a nearby table whose eyes were almost bulging out of his head. Grant stiffened. He wanted to smash his fist into the bastard's face, to smash something...

"I got caught up in doing too many things today," Crista said. "And I hadn't planned for that to happen." Her hand curled lightly against his chest. "I'd meant to do as you'd asked, buy myself something elegant and expensive that would make me fit in with these people, but—"

"But you couldn't bring yourself to do it," he said coldly. "It was much more important for you to make every man in the place go home tonight and dream of having you in his bed."

The crack of her hand against his cheek echoed through the ballroom like a clap of thunder.

Couples around them came to a stop and drew back, their eyes shining with anticipation, but the show was over.

Crista was already flying out the door. And Grant— Grant was going in the opposite direction, heading straight for the bar.

CHAPTER ELEVEN

THE intercom on Grant's desk buzzed. He frowned and ignored it but when it buzzed a second time, his frown became a scowl.

"Jane," he said as he punched the speaker button, "I told you I was not to be disturbed until Miss Madigan— Who?" Grant leaned back in his chair and began to smile. "Well, of course. Send him in."

He reached the door just as Cade came through it. The brothers hesitated, grinned, then threw their arms around each other.

"Cade, you son of a gun! Why didn't you let me know you were coming?"

"To tell you the truth, I didn't know it myself until a few hours ago." Cade smiled. "But when I realized I was going to be changing planes in New York, I figured, hey, could I touch down in this city and deny my big brother the chance to enjoy my presence for an evening?"

"One evening? That's it?"

"I'm afraid so, pal. We were in London when they ran into a problem in Dallas." Cade chuckled. "Not that a well coming in is a problem, you understand."

"A well? You mean that Texas oil company we were going to deep-six has struck oil?"

"You got it. There's some technical stuff needs the personal attention of the best oilman in the business—"

"You," Grant said, smiling.

"Who else?" Cade said with a modest grin. "So we booked ourselves on the first flight out of London, which meant landing here at Kennedy, and—"

"Slow down, buddy. Who's this 'we' you keep talking about?"

A slow flush spread across Cade's high cheekbones. "It's me—and, ah, and Angelica Gordon, the woman who headed up that company."

"You mean you offered her a job in London? But I thought she didn't know a damned thing about oil..." Grant's brows lifted as he looked at his brother's face. "Cade, you sly old fox."

"Grant." Cade's Adam's apple bounced up and down as he swallowed. "Grant—I'm—I'm getting married."

"You're what?"

"I'm getting married." Cade laughed self-consciously. "I know, I know. I can't believe it, either, but—hell, man, wait until you meet Angelica. You'll understand then. She's incredible. I mean, she's not just gorgeous. She's smart, and funny, and she knows me better than I know myself— Hey. What's the matter?"

"Nothing," Grant said. "I'm just—I'm surprised, that's all." He smiled and slapped his brother on the back. "Congratulations, and when do I get to offer my sympathies to the lady?"

"I told her to give us a couple of hours to talk man talk and then to meet us for dinner at that steak house over on East 54th. Is that okay—or do you have plans for the evening?"

Grant thought of Alicia Madigan, of her cool smile and eager sexuality, of how it had taken him the better part of a month to even consider giving her a phone call, and he smiled.

"Not a one," he said. He put his arm around Cade's shoulders and they walked out the door.

The lounge was a quiet, dimly lighted haven just off Third Avenue, and the brothers were on their second round in one of the rear booths before Cade cleared his throat and asked the question he'd been wanting to ask for the past hour.

"Listen," he said, "I hope I'm not out of line here, but—are you okay, Grant?"

Grant looked at Cade, saw the concern in his eyes, and decided to misunderstand the question.

"Sure." He managed what he hoped was a big smile. "Hey, just because we don't all get the chance to work out in the sun and develop year-round tans—"

"I talked to Zach. He said you'd called him a while back and that you didn't sound so hot."

"How's he doing? I can't believe he's still out on the West Coast—"

"I've got to tell you, you don't look so hot, either."

"Hey, I just told you, you've got this year-round tan while I—" The brothers' eyes met. After a moment, Grant shrugged. "I'm fine. Really. It's just that I had this deal that was driving me up the wall . . . You remember that thing of the old man's I got saddled with after he died?"

"The kid's guardianship?"

"Yes." Grant smiled tightly. "The only thing is, the 'kid' was all grown up. And I—she and I—we—"

"You got involved with her."

"Right. I knew it was wrong. Hell, the ethical and legal considerations of my position were—"

"Come on, don't give me a load of mumbo jumbo. What happened?"

Grant made damp circles on the tabletop with his ale mug.

"Nothing I'm terribly proud of. We—we had a thing going for a while and then I came to my senses and turned her over to somebody else."

Cade's brows lifted. "You turned her over to somebody else? You mean you introduced her to some guy and now she's sleeping with—hey!"

Grant had shot from his seat, grabbed his brother by the collar, and hauled him halfway across the scarred oak table before either man could blink. Now, he stared at Cade's stunned face and felt the blood drain from his own.

"Jesus," he whispered. "Cade, I'm sorry. I don't know what got into me. I've never—"

"No," Cade said. He sank back into the booth and grinned. "No, you never have. All the years we were growing up, when Zach and I got teed off at something, we'd toss a few punches at the wall or a bale of hay or even each other, but you were always Mr. Cool."

"Yeah." Grant looked at his trembling hands. "Hell," he muttered, wrapping them around his mug of ale, "the woman was bad news. I never lost my temper in my life until I met her, and then there didn't seem to be a day went by I wasn't yelling or cursing or grabbing her and—and—"

"Sounds to me like she did you a world of good," Cade said mildly.

"That's ridiculous. Civilized people don't—"

"Zach and I used to talk about it. You know, the way you were as fed up with the old man as we were but how you never flew off the handle. Me, I'd do a disappearing act, and Zach—Zach would pick a fight with every bozo who looked at him cross-eyed, but you?'' He shook his head. ''Hell, you never let the old man get to you, no matter how nasty he got.''

''It's just the way I was.''

''It's the way you made yourself, big brother. Only trouble is, you never got past it. I'd bet you never let a woman get under your skin—until this one.''

Grant wanted to deny it all, but what was the point? No woman had ever turned his world upside down and inside out, except Crista. It was a month—hell, it was four weeks, two days and five hours since she'd left him—and instead of thinking about her less, he thought about her more. How many times had he awakened in the dark of night and reached for her soft warmth?

But his bed was cold and empty, and so was his life. His elegant apartment felt more like a monochrome prison. He found himself looking for the brightness of her face and her clothing, listening for the tinkling sound of those tiny silver bells she'd worn in her ears, and a couple of days ago, walking along Lexington Avenue, he'd been horrified to find himself standing at a pet-shop window, smiling foolishly at the antics of a couple of puppies...

''Grant?''

He blinked. Cade was watching him, his eyes filled with compassion. Grant cleared his throat, did his best to choke out a laugh, and drank down the last of his ale.

''Okay, maybe she did dig under my hide a little, but in the final analysis, she was just a woman. Beautiful, yes. Smart as a whip. And—''

''You poor, dumb bastard,'' Cade said softly. ''You're in love with her!''

"In love? Me?" Grant tried to manage another laugh but this time he couldn't even come close. "Listen, Dr. Freud, I hate to disappoint you but— but..."

But what? Something within his chest seemed to expand. But what? he thought again.

"Why did you break it off?"

Grant shook his head. "It was just no good. I mean, she was—she's different. She's from Greenwich Village—she grew up there—and she designs jewelry and she's crazy about dogs and cats and—and—"

"Sounds like a real tough cookie to me," Cade said, trying not to smile, "the kind it would be hard to like."

"And then there was this guy—"

"Was she in love with him, or with you?"

"How the hell should I know?"

Cade grinned at the returning irritation in his brother's voice.

"Well, I suppose you might have asked her."

Grant stared at him. "You're right," he said slowly, "I guess I might have. But I didn't. I just got angry because—because..."

Dear God. He'd gotten angry because he'd been so crazy in love with Crista that the thought of letting her into his life had terrified him. It had been easier to shove her away than to run the risk of really caring...

Grant shot to his feet. "Listen," he said, "is there any chance you and—"

"Angelica."

"Right. Is there any chance you guys can hold over until tomorrow? I know you've got to get to Texas, but I'd really like to meet her and—"

"Go on." Cade smiled. "We'll be at the Plaza."

"Stay at my place." Grant dug into his pocket and tossed his keys on the table. "After all, my apartment looks more like a hotel than any hotel in town." He turned and started for the door, but Cade called him back.

"Hey, big brother." Cade got to his feet and held out his right hand, palm down. Grant grinned and laid his hand over it. "Remember," Cade said solemnly, "Deadeye Defenders never lose..."

"...no matter how tough a path they choose." Grant's smile faded. "I hope that's still true," he said softly.

Then he turned and hurried out of the lounge.

Crista was sitting at her kitchen table, carefully braiding three slender silver wires into one when the downstairs buzzer rang.

Annie gave a questioning bark and looked at her mistress.

"No, we're not expecting anyone," Crista said. "Somebody probably rang our bell by mistake."

The buzzer sounded again. Crista looked at the clock and frowned.

"It's too late for anyone to just drop by..."

Unless it were Danny. She put down the wire and her long-nosed pliers, gently pushed the one-eared cat from her lap, and got to her feet. Danny had moved out two weeks ago, but she'd told him to come by anytime to say hello.

The gray cat and the scrawny puppy followed her down the hall and watched as she pressed the wall buzzer.

It would be good to see Danny, she thought as she lifted Sweetness into her arms. He'd met someone and fallen head over heels in love—"just like in an old Preston Sturges flick," he'd said.

Crista was happy for him—and happy that he'd left. She still loved him like the big brother she'd never had, but he'd been driving her crazy with questions.

Like, how could she have ever thought herself in love with Grant Landon? And how could she still be in love with him after the way he'd treated her?

She didn't know how to answer the first without admitting to Danny what she hated admitting even to herself—that she'd been incredibly naive and talked herself into thinking sexual desire was love.

As for the second question—she'd sworn a thousand times that she wasn't in love with Grant, but Danny, who saw life through the frames of every sappy old movie ever made, refused to believe her.

"You're turning into a pile of skin and bones," he'd said, "and I hear you crying in your sleep. Crista, the guy's a jerk, and you ought to forget all about him."

Well, she was working on that. Danny just didn't understand. Dreaming about Grant didn't mean she still cared for him. People had bad dreams all the time.

Sooner or later, the dreams would go away. She'd meet someone else, a man she'd *really* fall in love with, and until then, she had a full, rich life to lead.

Annie yipped, stood on her hind legs, and pawed at Crista's skirt. She smiled, put the cat down, and took the puppy in her arms.

She had these two for family, she had volunteer work, and just last week, Mr. Abraham, who was the kind of guardian she should have had all along, had put his stamp of approval on the lease for a shop off Seventh Avenue with space in the back where she could design and make her jewelry, and plenty of room out front for her to display it.

The doorbell rang. Crista smiled, put Annie down on the floor, and flung open the door.

"Danny," she said with a big smile, "I'm so glad you're back. Give me a big kiss and..." Her hand flew to her throat. "Grant?"

"Hello, Crista."

She stared at him while her heart thudded painfully in her breast. He looked just as she remembered him, as she'd dreamed of him, big and broad-shouldered and sternly, magnificently masculine.

"May I come in?"

Everything in her was telling her to slam the door in his face—but Annie was dancing excitedly around his legs and even Sweetness was rubbing his head against Grant's ankle.

She, at least, could manage to be polite.

"Yes," she said coolly, and she stepped aside and let him pass.

She shut the door and stood behind him, watching as he looked slowly around the cramped living room.

"You don't seem to have changed anything," he said.

She took a breath, stepped briskly around him, and made her way to the kitchen.

"No. Why would I?"

"Well, I thought, with your inheritance—"

"The money hasn't changed me," she said more sharply than she'd intended. "I'm still the same person I always was."

He looked at her. She was wearing a royal blue skirt embroidered with silver stars, a long-sleeved white sweater, and a silver vest. The tiny bells he loved swayed from her earlobes.

But it was her face he looked at the longest. That beautiful face, with its violet eyes, its soft, sweet mouth, its determined chin...

"Yes," he said quietly, and smiled, "yes, you are the same person you always were." His smile dimmed. "But you're thinner. You've lost weight, haven't you?"

A shudder went through her. Don't look at me like that, she thought, please, don't...

She straightened, wrapped her arms around herself, and gave him a cold look.

"Why have you come here, Grant? If it's some bit of legal nonsense you overlooked, I'd prefer you to take it up with Sam Abraham."

"Are you in such a rush to get rid of me?" he said softly.

Her eyes flew to his. No, she thought, oh no, I don't want to get rid of you. I want you to stay, I want— I want...

"I gather you're waiting for Danny to come home."

Crista turned quickly and took the kettle from the stove.

"I—yes," she said, filling it with water, "that's right. He's—he's out, and—and—"

"Do you love him?"

Grant's voice was harsh, filled with the anger he felt. No, he thought, no, it wasn't anger. It was—it was pain.

"Answer me, dammit!" His hands closed hard on her shoulders. "Do you love him, Crista?"

She closed her eyes and carefully put the kettle on the countertop.

"Go away," she said, her voice trembling despite all her efforts to keep it cool and steady. "If you've any decency in you, Grant, please, go away."

His hands tightened on her as he turned her un-yielding body toward him. His hand went under her chin and tilted it up until she was looking at his face.

His eyes were so dark. And he had lost weight, too; she could see the fine, hard bones standing out under his taut skin. Crista began to tremble. She wanted to lift her hands, lay them against his cheeks, bring his mouth down to hers...

Tears rose in her eyes. Please, she thought, please, God, don't do this to me...

But it was too late. Her lonely, aching heart was beating out the truth, telling her what she had known all along—that she loved Grant, that she adored him, and that she always would.

Grant saw the tears fill her eyes, saw her mouth begin to tremble, and his heart turned over in his chest.

"Crista?" he whispered.

"Please." Her breath whispered on a long, in-drawn sigh. "Please, just—just go away. Just—"

He took her face in his hands, bent to her, and kissed her. It was a kiss filled with tenderness, and sweetness, and all the love that had so long been walled within his heart.

"Crista," he said, "I love you."

Her eyes flew to his.

"If—if Danny means more to you than I do, I'll—I'll wish you happiness and walk out that door." He took a deep breath. "But I can't believe you love him, not after what we shared. I have to believe, with all my heart, that I'm the only man you want, the man you'll spend your life with."

The tears that shone in her eyes spilled down her cheeks.

"Oh, Grant! Grant, I love you so much!" She gave a sobbing laugh as his arms went around her. "I've always loved you, only you. Don't you know that?"

"But Danny..."

"The only thing I ever shared with Danny was this apartment."

"I don't understand. You said—"

"*You* said. You said he was my lover, and I let you think it. But he's never been anything to me but a friend." She took a breath. "There's never been anyone but you, Grant. You're the first man I ever loved—the first I ever made love with."

Grant crushed her lips beneath his. After a long time, he lifted his head.

"Crista, sweetheart, can you ever forgive me? I think I must have fallen in love with you the minute I saw you—"

"The minute I ran you down, you mean."

He smiled, and then he sighed. "I was just so afraid of letting myself feel anything that—hell, I lied to myself." His arms tightened around her. "When you left me, I felt as if my life had drained away."

"I'll never leave you again," she whispered. "Never!"

They kissed until a faint "yip" drew them apart.

"I see the shelter managed to find Annie a good home," Grant said, laughing as he bent down and scratched the puppy's ears.

"I hadn't intended to keep her," Crista said. "You'd asked me not to, and I knew how you felt about cats and dogs, and—"

He straightened up and took her in his arms again. "You know, I've been thinking about redecorating my apartment." His brow furrowed. "But I'm going to need expert advice. I mean, I've no idea what fabrics go best with cat and dog fur.''

Crista laughed and curled her arms around Grant's neck.

''Well, you've come to the right place for help. I'm definitely an expert in the field.''

''It has to be a scheme that will suit my wife, as well. She's a woman who likes colorful things, and she'll need a workroom of some sort where she can design jewelry...''

Crista smiled. ''All your wife will ever need is right here, in her arms,'' she sighed, her lips inches from Grant's.

Grant's hands slipped into her hair. ''And that's where you're going to stay, because I'm never going to lose you again. I'll love you forever, my darling,'' he promised.

And she knew, without question, that it was true.

* * * * *

If you enjoyed this book, watch out next month for HOLLYWOOD WEDDING *by Sandra Marton, in which we meet Grant's brother Zach—and Eve, a most unexpected ''mistress''...*

BRIDE'S BAY RESORT

UNLOCK THE DOOR TO GREAT ROMANCE AT BRIDE'S BAY RESORT

Join Harlequin's new across-the-lines series, set in an exclusive hotel on an island off the coast of South Carolina.

Seven of your favorite authors will bring you exciting stories about fascinating heroes and heroines discovering love at Bride's Bay Resort.

Look for these fabulous stories coming to a store near you beginning in January 1996.

Harlequin American Romance #613 in January
Matchmaking Baby by Cathy Gillen Thacker

Harlequin Presents #1794 in February
Indiscretions by Robyn Donald

Harlequin Intrigue #362 in March
Love and Lies by Dawn Stewardson

Harlequin Romance #3404 in April
Make Believe Engagement by Day Leclaire

Harlequin Temptation #588 in May
Stranger in the Night by Roseanne Williams

Harlequin Superromance #695 in June
Married to a Stranger by Connie Bennett

Harlequin Historicals #324 in July
Dulcie's Gift by Ruth Langan

Visit Bride's Bay Resort each month wherever Harlequin books are sold.

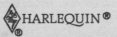

HARLEQUIN®

BBAYG

Take 4 bestselling love stories FREE

Plus get a FREE surprise gift!

You're About to Become a
Privileged
Woman

Reap the rewards of fabulous free gifts and
benefits with proofs-of-purchase from
Harlequin and Silhouette books

Pages & Privileges™

It's our way of thanking you for
buying our books at your
favorite retail stores.

Harlequin and Silhouette—
the most privileged readers in the world!

For more information about Harlequin and
Silhouette's PAGES & PRIVILEGES program call the
Pages & Privileges Benefits Desk: 1-503-794-2499

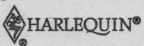